ALL DOWN THE LINE

ANDREW J FIELD

Published by Hit the North
Mill Wharf
Tweedmouth
Berwick upon Tweed
Northumberland
TD15 2BP

First published by Boomslang Books in 2020.

This revised/rewritten 2025 version, based on the original novel, follows a similar narrative arc and the same characters.

ISBN: 9781068574771

Also

Without Rules

After the Bridge

'Manchester is the only English City which
can look London in the face, not merely as a
regional capital but as a rival version of how
man should live in a community.'
AJP Taylor

'Everyone has a plan until
they get punched in the mouth.'
Mike Tyson & Nick Forti

All
Down
the
Line

Based on an untrue story

WAITING AROUND TO DIE

Waiting Around to Die is a song by an American singer songwriter Townes Van Zandt. I saw him perform this cheerful ditty in a boozer in Bury. Less than a dozen punters in a tiny upstairs room listening to an intoxicated wreck crying on stage between sad songs and overlong jokes. That was a few years before he died of a heart attack, aged fifty-two. Now, he is more famous dead than alive. That song always struck a chord with me. We're all *Desperadoes Waiting for a Train* (another great tune by Townes' melancholic mate, Guy Clark, also obsessed with hanging around until he kicked the bucket). Our departure to the other side is inevitable, just a matter of when and how you cross the line...

One
Castlefield, Manchester, 3rd September 2017

The bell rings inside his head, showtime kicks off in a couple of minutes. He feels edgy, sips chilled Chablis to soothe his nerves, no time to sneak outside for a calming tab. He adjusts his backside in the dentist's chair, half hidden in the corner of the Red Manifesto, a glam Pan-American diner he co-owns. They are seconds away from being crowned restaurant of the year by the Manchester Daily News. Winning a gong is tidy, but his personal pitch is more important. He is planning to propose to April Sands, in his eyes the most talented and beautiful woman in the world.

Big question: does she want to be his next new wife?

April stands tall next to svelte food critic Grace Stark, infamous in her own lunchtime for never turning down second helpings of puddings, or anything else she can swallow. What Grace doesn't know about scoffing could be scribbled in shorthand on a bumble bee's left nut. Grace graciously hands April a large heavy trophy, a bronze capital M embedded into a square wooden plate like an axe swung hard at a tree trunk. Smiling, April thanks Manchester's finest for naming them the city's favourite place to dine out.

'This time next year we want a Michelin star.'

Everybody laughs. They aren't Michelin star people, never want to be. The Red Manifesto is synonymous with a good time, a place where punters don't have to take out a second mortgage for a ten-course taster menu before buying chips and gravy on the way home.

April milks the applause, hands the trophy back to Grace who steps away, waits until the clapping subsides and looks lovingly in his direction.

'There are lots of people involved in the Red Manifesto project who can take great pride in this award, but none more so than my business partner and best friend, Cain Bell. Please, join me on the stage.'

'No, it's your moment,' he deadpans from the dentist's chair. He stands up and takes several long strides towards her. 'Your achievement. Your idea. Your hard work. You are the creative genius behind the Manifesto.'

'Without you, it's nothing,' she replies. 'Your PR skills shine the light on our collective mission to disrupt Manchester dining.'

He looks at April, his eyes and his mind are focused on the big question.

'Will you marry me?'

The guests are transfixed. April says nothing. Did he speak loudly and clearly enough?

'Yes, I'll marry you, darling,' says a deep-voiced male wag he doesn't recognise, squeezing out a predictable laugh, pretending to accept his offer.

'You're the guy, Cain,' says crime reporter Matt Stark, his

oldest best mate and Grace's better half. What stick insect Matt doesn't know about his two obsessions — criminals and cask ale — can be touch-typed on forementioned bumble bee's other nut. Matt is his first choice for best man, although Cain hasn't popped the question to him yet.

Cain navigates the chairs and tables between the bar and the stage and self-doubts kicks in. He and April have never discussed marriage in their two short years together. They have been too busy having fun to think about the future. In their hedonistic world, they see themselves as Mancunian versions of Bogart and Bacall, Burton and Taylor, Sinatra and Gardener, a glam couple living it large under a massive spinning mirror ball, although she is far more famous than him.

In fact, nobody will blame April if she turns Cain down. She is an international celebrity chef with a literary agent for her books and another for TV work. A female Anthony Bourdain without the substance abuse, stress and anxiety that often accompanies fame. Cain tells his mates he's a cut-price Charles Bukowski, a taller northern barfly without the former post office man's drink problem, literary skills and bank balance. He stalks her shadow, tab in hand, relying on his wits to keep the wolves at bay. Not that he minds if she owns ninety percent of the business to his ten. His life manifesto is the same as *Saturday Night and Sunday Morning's* Arthur Seaton, who claims in his naivety that his only truth is having a good time, the rest is just propaganda. Arthur's a bit of a shit but it is still the best opening to a film, ever.

Cain drops lightly onto one knee, holds April's hand in his, hopes their eye contact will inspire a quick answer and repeats the question.

'Will you be my wife?'

'Where's the ring? You're meant to give her a bloody ring,' shouts Vince Crane, the Red Manifesto's giant Irish head of security, his newest best mate and an alternative best man pick. Cain has only known Vince two years since they'd opened the Manifesto, but they bonded immediately. They like the same indie music, like the same team dressed in red, like the same booze poured black and slow and like the same bitter-sweet macho banter. Cain calls anything Irish *diddly* and Vince finds that hilarious rather than racist.

There is more laughter, and Cain pretends he has clean forgotten the ring; his simple man act is never taking life too seriously. A small velvet box containing a five grand princess cut diamond solitaire ring set in 18 carat yellow gold shows the opposite is true. Is it sparkly enough to win a gorgeous gal's heart? Cain is about to find out.

'Yes,' she says.

Does Cain hear her right? Yes, she does, or yes, she doesn't? He has the box in his hand. Lifts the lid, takes the engagement ring out, places it gently on April's finger. Naturally, it fits perfectly, like he knows it will. He doesn't leave things to chance.

'A token of my unconditional love.'

'Yes. I'll be honoured to be your wife, Mr Cain Bell. The ring is beautiful, must have cost you an arm and a leg.'

'You are worth every limb,' he quips, quick as a flash, the self-deprecating king of the pre-planned spontaneous one-liner.

Applause bounces off the exposed brick walls of the former waterside warehouse. They kiss; phones capture the moment. Images and videos posted, liked and shared on social media the instant their lips touch, her left hand cupping his face, showing off her engagement ring. April adjusts herself slightly and leans into Cain, speaks only for his ears.

'Ted Blake didn't kill Hannah.'

She pulls away, breaks the embrace. Cain is gutted,

kicked in the nuts. Has he misheard or has she misspoken? His planned speech about the depth of their love sinks like a lead balloon.

Cain is gobsmacked. As far as he is aware, only four people knew Ted Blake was behind the wheel. One is him, obviously. Two others — his daughter, the victim, Hannah, and her killer, Ted Blake — are dead. The fourth is detective inspector Len Harvey, a human wrecking ball as wide as he is tall, an outsized Johnny Cash lookalike who calls everyone *son*. Harvey introduced Cain to a cancer-ridden Blake. The latter confessed on his death bed that he hit Cain's eleven-year-old at fifty miles an hour at a pelican crossing on Bury New Road in Prestwich. That was the same weekend a drunk driver crashed a Mercedes Benz into a tunnel wall in Paris, France, and immortalised Lady Di, the nation's Queen of Hearts who, like dear old Marilyn Monroe, masochist Jimmy Dean, belligerent Ronnie Van Zant and cramping Kurt Cobain, will never grow old and decrepit.

Officially, the driver was never caught, the car with false number plates never found, the police never even had one suspect and nobody was ever interviewed. Friends were amazed Cain wasn't angrier, but they didn't know the full story.

Only four people did, until now.

For twenty years Cain believed Blake's account because he said Hannah wore a little red dress and carried a giant Domino's pizza box as she crossed the road towards the Forrester's and the precinct. Several times Cain begged Harvey to arrest Blake so he could have his day in court, but the police detective grunted that a secret confession was as good as it was going to get, telling him to be grateful for small mercies. Blake would be dead before a jury ever got to hear any circumstantial evidence and might even allow him to walk free if they felt sorry for him with stage 4 terminal cancer and a young baby girl about to lose her father. On a personal level, Harvey was going out on a limb by giving Cain a name and, with it, definitive closure. If Harvey was ever caught, he would lose everything, his job, his pension, his future. Cain had to swear blind never to talk about Ted Blake to anyone, ever.

Now, according to Cain's future wife's unsolicited revelation, he is a big time April fool. Who else was complicit by their deadly silence? Although Cain and Big Len were close before Cain left Manchester six months after Hannah's death, they haven't caught up since he returned from his self-imposed overseas exile. Cain kids himself that opening a restaurant and building a brand from scratch meant he never had the time to rekindle their friendship.

That is a big lie, that is Cain being disingenuous.

Cain stays away from Harvey and his merry men drinking buddies because they remind him of what he's lost. At the same time, Harvey has ignored Cain's homecoming and never made any attempt to hook up with him. Not that their mutual estrangement matters. Cain will soon find out what really happened when he hears April's explanation. If it wasn't Ted Blake, then Cain wants the name of the bastard bloke behind the wheel who ruined his life and left him an empty shell of a man he once dreamed of being. Isn't much to ask, no matter how much the truth hurts. Cain wants to look the man square in the eyes and hear him apologise for the endless grief and pain. Is that *sorry* enough? He will find out when Hannah's murderer is exposed by April.

Two

Naturally, Cain wants to cut the celebrations short to hear April explain why she has decided to make Ted Blake headline news again. He stops drinking and is ready to go home to hear her true confessions. Unfortunately, his new fiancée does not share his desire for a speedy exit and networks with the Red Manifesto's minted guests without a care in the world, until she locks horns with psychiatrist Lucy Button, nicknamed Doll Face on account of her heroin-chic similarity to prime-time Debbie Harry, Blondie's lead singer. They are mates, members of the Red Manifesto Double TT Bookclub, a group of expensively dressed ladies of leisure who like to drink wine and chat about literature, and anything else that fires their imaginations over extended lunch gatherings on Tuesdays and Thursdays. Without warning their friendly chat sours when April and Lucy exchange face slaps. Nobody notices apart from Cain and Vince Crane.

'What do you want me to do?'

'Empty this place,' Cain says.

The confrontation between the restauranteur and the shrink is over before it starts, and they walk away in opposite directions. Are they arguing about Cain? Lucy counselled him on the couch and in her bed after Hannah's death. Is she a jealous queen? Don't be daft, not every soap opera revolves around Cain bloody Bell.

'Give us quarter of an hour to lock up — I'll walk with you along the canal path,' says Vince, who is better connected in Manchester than the national grid. His job is to keep the Red Manifesto free from trouble, no drugs, no hookers, no wankers, no gangsters, no questions about his methods.

Although Vince lives in the Manchester's trendy Northern Quarter, his usual practice is to escort the Red Manifesto owners back to their apartment by car when it is wet and miserable or on foot when it is dry and magnificent. Occasionally, he asks for a free pass when a woman is on the hunt. Tonight, Lucy Button, left razor-bone cheek redder than the right after playing slap, slinks towards them like a panther on heat.

'Vince, fancy getting feral again?' she asks, as subtle as a sledgehammer cracking a nut.

'Are you and April OK?' Cain asks her.

'Menopause,' she replies.

'Yours or hers?'

'Still as sharp as a blunt knife, Cain,' says Lucy.

'Silly question. Sorry. I know you never talk about your clients.'

'Complete confidentiality, guaranteed, including you, Cain.'

'Pleased to hear it,' Cain says.

'I might be writing my memoirs one day, you'll be in them,' says Lucy, winking gratuitously, salaciously.

'Promise to make me look good,' says Cain.

'That might be too tall an ask,' says Lucy, 'Congratulations, by the way.'

'You kept that quiet,' says Vince.

'Ditto, you two love birds.'

'Nice ring,' says Vince, ignoring the quip about him and Lucy. 'How much?'

'Five,' Cain replies.

'Mind if I skip escort duties?'

'Is it raining?'

'In Manchester?'

'We're not called *Rainy City* without good reason,' Cain replies, even if the city's reputation for excessive rain is a myth perpetuated by PR people like him. There are lots of UK cities and towns wetter, but why let the truth spoil a good story?

'Dry as the Sahara Desert between Margaret Thatcher's legs...the perfect evening for a romantic stroll for two love cats.'

'Thanks for putting that image in my head, Vince,' Cain says. 'Thatcher's thatch is enough to put me off sex for life.'

Vince is obsessed with the ex-Conservative Prime Minister who was never for turning, no matter what the consequences. He would regularly denigrate her, even when the iron lady's rusted, her demented mind dancing with the fairies.

'My pleasure,' he says. 'Enjoy your walk. Never forget Thatcher willingly starved wee Bobby Sands, MP, to death. Not just him. Francis, Raymond, Patsy, Joe, Martin, Kevin and Kieran too. Only one of them over thirty years of age, the rest snotty nosed kids in their twenties. Hope she is burning in hell for eternity for what she did to them and their families and friends.'

By the time Lucy powders her nose, Crane clears the restaurant. Cain and April watch the duo race away in his black Range Rover. They drive left up Castle Street rather than right towards St John Street where Doll Face lives in an apartment above her clinic. Maybe they are picking up recreational treats on the way home? If they are, it is nothing to do with Cain. Vince is an adult off the Red Manifesto clock when his shift ends, and Lucy is her own gal. She is entitled to bed hop same way bees promiscuously flit from flower-to-flower filching pollen.

April and Cain start their leisurely ten-minute waterside stroll along the Rochdale Canal towards their 42nd floor city centre penthouse, the tallest residential building outside of London. The skyscraper dominates northern Deansgate, but other even bigger giant buildings are in the pipeline, ready to transform Manchester's skyline. On the plus side, more cash rich punters munching, supping and sipping in the Manifesto is good for the bottom line. On the negative, Manchester is selling its soul to the highest bidder, prioritising profits over people, the dirty old town castrated by outsiders with deep pockets.

'Phew,' says April. 'That was a long exhausting night.'

'I saw your handbags at dawn with Doll Face. Anything you want to share?' Cain asks.

Cain lights a tab and inhales deeply. Like all former smokers, April hates smoking and bans him from chuffing indoors at home and work. She turns her head away to avoid inhaling second hand smoke.

'No.'

'Nothing.'

'Ted Blake?'

'At home.'

'Shall I take that?' Cain gestures to the heavy award with his cigarette, the burning butt a firefly dancing in the moonlight. 'Difficult to hold, tougher to carry over distance.'

'No. I like prizes.'

'Like me?'

'Like you.'

Cain bends down and flicks the half-smoked tab into the water. Softly, softly, does it. They kiss. Lips brush. They kiss more intimately. Tongues touch. But the spark is missing. Cain stops. He needs to know right now, he cannot wait a second longer.

'Ted Blake?'

'Not here. At home. How many times...?'

She charges off down the towpath, water to the left, walls covered in graffiti to the right. Cain reaches out to grab her arm. She slips his grasp, resists his attempts to stop her walking away.

'Tell me about Ted Blake NOW?'

At the third time of asking she stops; Cain's hands gently touch her shoulders for reassurance. Her lips start to move; a word forms. Before it is uttered, her mouth adopts a different shape, her eyes distracted by activity behind him.

'What's going on?'

There is no time for an answer. Cain's legs go from under him, and he is tumbling. He expects to land on cold concrete with a painful bang, but belly flops into cold canal water. The air expels from his lungs. Is he having a heart attack or a catastrophic stroke? He spits out mouthfuls of muddy water, sucks in air to fill his lungs, doggy paddles to stay afloat, conscious that waterlogged jeans, a suede jacket, black tee and imitation RM McWilliam crocodile boots can pull him under.

He is a tall man, and he can test the depth of the water by simply standing but the canal bottom is littered with broken glass bottles and used syringes and is not worth the risk.

Combined cadet force swimming lessons kick in, and Cain rolls on to his back, pushes his stomach out and extends his arms and legs into a star shape.

He gently moves hands and feet to help him float so he can assess his situation. He checks to see if April is marinading in the murky brown broth with him.

'April, are you OK? Where are you?'

Cain looks up, a lanky thug wearing a full-face-balaclava towers above him in the silvery glow of the moonlight, a Nazi swastika beauty spot the size of a two-pound coin is tattooed on his exposed right cheek below his eye. The dark ink insignia makes the balaclava disguise redundant, brands him stupid as well as psychopathic.

'Stay,' Swastika Boy sneers, and contemptuously spits in the water. He repeats his instruction several times, armed with the heavy restaurant of the year award that he holds aloft like the FA Cup, ready to throw at the slightest provocation.

A voice from the far side of the waterway yells, 'get him out of the water.' A dog howls in the distance and others wail in canine solidarity.

A distracted Swastika Boy looks to see who has the audacity to interrupt his fun. He looks back towards the city centre, the source of the howling and the wailing. He glances towards April and turns to Cain and hurls the award straight at his head. Cain ducks under and hopes for the best but waits for the pain and the agony.

There is none. Swastika Boy misses.

Cain resurfaces and hears a loud splash. He has company in the water. Within seconds an arm holds him by his shoulders, swims with him to the side of the canal with the ease of a professional lifeguard.

'Stay there. It's very slippery,' says Cain's rescuer, scrambling out of the water using the metal railings by the towpath. He effortlessly scales the slippery brickwork, his strong hands reach down to grab Cain.

By the time Cain is out of the water, the mugging is over, and Swastika Boy is monkey-walking towards Deansgate, aping the gait of his taller companion as they both pull off their balaclavas.

April scrambles on the ground and appears unharmed as she retrieves the contents of her handbag.

'You OK, love? Did you lose consciousness?' asks their Good Samaritan, holding up two fingers. 'How many fingers do you see?'

'Three of them,' April says, after a slight delay.

'Two or three fingers?' He does it again, his gnarled knuckles at odds with their strength.

This time she gets it right.

'Two.'

'You sure you didn't pass out?' Cain asks.

'No.'

Cain feels his pockets for his mobile and realises it is lost on the bottom of the canal, a grand down the drain. A Marlboro Red soft pack survives the impromptu dip, but the soaked coffin sticks are about as useful as a chocolate fireguard. His suede jacket and RM McWilliam brown imitation croc boots are ruined too, another thousand quid washed away.

'What did they steal?'

'Nothing,' she smiles. 'Just want to go home, you two need to get dry before you catch a cold.'

Cain takes her word nothing is missing, glad it has only been an expensive bit of push and shove, nothing too violent. She is slightly shaken, but essentially unmarked, a barely noticeable slight bump on her temple or is that purely in Cain's overactive imagination. The moonlight gives everything an artificial silvery sheen.

'What happened? My name is Nick.'

Cain gives Nick the once over. He is missing his two front teeth. Up close he looks familiar, but Cain cannot place him in the silver half-light.

'I'll call Vince. He'll teach them a lesson they'll never forget.'

'Will he?' asks April.

'I'll call the cops,' Nick says. 'Can I borrow your mobile?'

'No police. And no Vince. Where do you live, Nick?' April asks, ignoring Cain and the request for a phone.

Nick nods at a small group of tents in the shadow of the skyscraper. Cain has passed the chaotic camp numerous times and never really clocked homeless folk living an off-grid waterside existence while he swanned around Manchester like he was special.

'She should go to A&E. Her mince pies are scrambled,' says Nick.

Although Nick is concerned about her eyes, Cain knows she is blind in one eye, a detached retina stops her driving. She keeps her disability a secret because she isn't a bleeding heart wanting to be swamped in self-pity. Ditto the hysterectomy that prevents her from having more children after the twins, Summer and stillborn Eric.

Cain wants to reassure her, but she shrugs him away when he tries to put an arm around her shoulders. Less than an hour after agreeing to be his wife, she is disconnecting.

How deep is their love? He'll find out as soon as they clean up Nick and thank him. More hanging around, but Cain doesn't mind, as long as April tells him the name of the man responsible for his daughter's death. He's been conned for twenty-years, another sixty minutes isn't going to kill him.

Three

Cain offers Nick the choice of a very late supper or an early morning breakfast washed down with Tom Oliver's world famous 'minimal intervention' Herefordshire natural cider. Cain is old school about saying thank you and Nick deserves a decent spread. Without his intervention April and Cain might be in A&E counting lost teeth and stitches or setting broken bones and repairing damaged internal organs. Not that April shares his enthusiasm. They enter the penthouse apartment, and she disappears into a bedroom without a word.

'Grub for Nick?'

There is still no answer, so Cain slides Nick a bottle of Tom's cider and opens one himself, oblivious to the fact he is adding more grease to the frying pan plying an alcoholic with alcohol.

With April otherwise engaged, Cain ignores her towpath

instructions and calls Vince. The Irishman does not answer. Despite her various addictions, Lucy Button has a healthy appetite for shagging, as Cain knows from personal experience. He leaves a simple message: mugged by a thug with a Swastika tattoo on his cheek. Call me ASAP. Vince might be too busy tonight, but he can sort it out tomorrow with a few slaps, no questions asked.

For a second he thinks about calling detective Len Harvey to demand the truth about Ted Blake. He logs onto his iPad in the kitchen, finds Harvey's mobile number in the contacts app where it has been safely stored in the cloud for two decades, but decides to delay while Nick is his guest.

'Cheers.'

'Cheers.'

'Thank you.'

'No worries.'

Cain and Nick sip their cider and strip naked and sip some more. Cain gathers the wet clothes, shoves them in the washer and presses the start button for a forty-seven-minute wash. He grabs a couple of bathroom towels from the airing cupboard, wraps one around his midriff, hands the other to Nick and notices a raging black-green Thor tattooed on his back, the Norse God's trademark hammer raised high above his head. The recognition bell rings out loud, Cain has a genuine celebrity on the 42nd floor penthouse, fists full of dynamite.

'You're Nick 'Thor' Forti?'

'I was.'

'Now?'

'A drunk,' replies Nick, toasting Cain with his half empty bottle of Oliver's.

Cain can remember Nick boxing back in the day at the Willows in Salford, a ring warrior surrounded by squealing wild pigs, Côtes du Rhône and blood splashed on starched white dress shirts and colourful evening gowns.

'We can't thank you enough.'

'You'd have done it for me.'

'Of course,' Cain lies. 'How did you end up homeless?'

'Shagging around. Kylie took everything, except my drink habit.'

'You tried AA?'

'Several times. The God bit does my head in.'

Instinctively, guiltily, Cain grabs April's handbag and takes the petty cash from the envelope and starts counting. There is a couple of grand — two-thousand-one-hundred and forty-five is written on the envelope. Normally April puts the cash in her safe hidden in a fitted wardrobe in the master bedroom. She says all her valuables, jewellery, her passport, flat deeds, numerous shares and legal certificates and contingency cash are stashed away out of reach and out of mind. She says she knows she is ultra cautious, but thieves are attracted to rich people like flies to cow pats so the combination safe is brilliantly disguised as a shoe cupboard within a cupboard. Although Cain has never looked inside the safe out of respect for her privacy, he knows the combination: the same as her mobile. Weird really, four numbers open-up her world. Unlike April, Cain's life is stored in a brown leather man-bag, the size of a decent hardcover crime fiction novel like James Ellroy's *American Tabloid*, his favourite novel of all time, reimagining the Kennedy assassination two years before Cain was born.

'What's the hourly rate for a hero?'

Cain immediately feels crass. Twice in a couple of minutes he's been a complete knob. Maybe he is in shock without realising and is unable to think straight?

'I don't want your money. If you want to pay anyone, give some cash to my ex-wife, Kylie Forti, and my son, Noel, and daughter, Molly, 25a Princess Charlotte Street, Radcliffe. No worries if you don't. You should take her to hospital. I ought to be going. Have you got any spare sports clobber?'

Cain steps into the home gym next to the kitchen. Grabs spare sports clothes, shorts and track suit tops. Throws them at Nick. He puts them to one side, realising they both still stink of dirty old canals.

'Thanks. Snazzy threads, they'll help me pull the chicks, no problem.'

'Sorry for interrupting your evening.'

'Don't worry about it,' says Nick. 'Everybody has a plan until they get punched in the mouth.'

'That's a great line. Original?'

'Yes, although Mike Tyson heard me say it and claimed it as his own. He punches too hard and is too big for me to argue with him.'

'You've met Mike Tyson?'

'A few times. At shows. He was my hero when he was at the top of his game. The rape and prison time and the drugs and bankruptcy not so impressive,' says Nick.

'He's doing OK now?'

'Depends on your definition. Fighting is a loser's game. Look what happens to street fighting men — even the best of us. Heroin addict Joe Louis was in a wheelchair, paranoid and demented, listening to talking radiators. The only way unloved Sonny Liston, a drunk and a junky, was leaving Vegas was in a wooden box owned by the mob. Look at Ali, his brains and body trashed to enrich others. They treat dogs better.'

'My favourite boxing quote is Sonny talking about the price of pugilism: someday they'll write a blues song just for fighters. It'll be for a slow guitar, soft trumpet and a bell. That's some epitaph for pugilists,' says Cain.

Nick laughs and rasps in the same breath, his voice shot from living in concrete city in the cold and the damp.

'Don't fall for the hardman mythology. Liston was a nasty bully and probably a rapist too, like Tyson. In Sonny's defence, he died the day he was born. Never stood a chance. Black, poor and illiterate. Took him an age to sign his signature. Never could read or write like normal people. Even we rejected him as a role model. Swap Arkansas for Radcliffe and my life story was his. Any black boxer's story.'

'Think he dived in the Ali fights?'

'Everyone has a price.'

'Did you?'

'I accepted an offer once. I was going to take a dive, but my silly pride stopped me. They can have my body and my mind, but never my heart,' says Nick, punctuating his point by beating the left side of his chest with his right fist.

'Who?'

'You don't want to know,' says Nick through tight lips, probably still hacked off at the thought of taking a fall for a few extra quid. 'I am saving naming names until I write my life story like my mate Ricky Hatton, not that I am anywhere near as famous or as fat as him.'

'Does it still hurt, being bossed about?' asks Cain.

'Not anymore. Boxing is a cruel and vicious sport unlike any other. The more vicious the more people enjoy it. In boxing the intent is to maim. When a guy gets cut, the opponent goes to work on it trying to make it worse and people watching are yelling, kill him, knock him down. They have a lust for violence, and they have a lust for blood, as long as isn't their own. I am a free man now people cannot make any more money out of me.'

There is a pause in the chat. Bribery and buying a working man's dignity can kill an interesting boxing conversation stone dead. Nick is right about so-called hardmen, Cain isn't interested in celebrating violent gangsters. They are good cinema box office, charismatic cartoon characters, nothing else. Away from the silver screen, they are best avoided like sexuality transmitted infections.

'Weren't you ever worried about killing your opponent in the ring?'

'It was always him or me. You ever boxed?' asks Nick.

'I am lover not a fighter,' Cain jokes.

'I was both,' he says, and finishes his bottle of cider without asking for another. 'But they are not comfortable bed companions, loving and fighting. Can I have a shower?'

'The shower is next to the home gym. The towels are clean. I'll go check on April, she's very quiet.'

Cain moves towards the corridor, waits while he composes himself. He has to play it cool, doesn't want to come across as a meathead bully picking on a woman. There are plenty of men enjoying a free ride from family, friends, colleagues and the media. Several beats pass before he enters the bedroom.

'Are you going to come and say goodbye to Nick?'

Cain is talking to an empty room, so he knocks on the en suite door to avoid intruding on April's privacy. Again, there is no answer, and he gently pushes the mirrored door. It barely moves, there is an obstruction. He pushes one more time, harder, with more conviction. Manages to shift the door, until it is slightly ajar. Through the crack, he peers into the bathroom. Sees April out cold, spreadeagled naked on the marble tiled floor, lying on her back. White ming is frothing around her mouth.

'How long have you been lying there?'

She doesn't move or respond, she is unconscious, possibly dead. Not again. Lightning doesn't strike twice, unless your name is Cain bloody Bell, and you are born double unlucky.

Four

Cain has been here before when his daughter flew down Bury New Road, Prestwich, after being hit on a pelican crossing by a black Golf. His mind blanked out then as it does now. His bare feet are frozen to the warm marble floor. He tries to yell for help, calls out April's name as loud as he can. His lips and tongue move, but he hears no sound, apart from a howling wolf's primal scream so loud he covers his ears to no avail. The noise is still deafening.

'What's up?' asks Nick. He bursts into the bathroom, naked body dripping with soapy water. 'Heard you shout.'

'Look.'

Nick sinks to his knees and inspects April's face, slapping her cheeks gently like a baby's bottom.

'April, wake up. It's Nick. We met earlier tonight. Wake up.'

There is no response. Cain hears a voice ask if she is

breathing. It sounds a lot like his, but he is rooted to the spot. Nick grabs Cain's shaving mirror and holds it under her nose to check if the glass mists up.

'Is she?'

'I think she's still breathing. Call an ambulance.'

'What?'

Cain still cannot move. Nick jumps up, yanks the towel from around his waist, leaving all three of them naked.

'You're in shock. I've seen boxers with bad head injuries. You must act fast, no time for messing, every second is important. Tell 999 she has had a bad fall, banged her head hard, lost consciousness. Could be a serious brain injury. Don't downplay it or they'll ignore us and leave us in a queue for hours. We want to be their number one priority,' he says, using Cain's towel as a cushion to slightly elevate April's head.

Where is Cain's mobile? He'd lost it in the canal when they were mugged. He would use April's. Where is it? Her handbag in the kitchen? Or on the bed with her clothes? It is the former. Cain grabs the device and keys in April's four-digit code on the iPhone 8 Plus. His digital passcode is the same as hers. They share everything, like lovers do.

Cain hears somebody calmly telling the ambulance operator they suspect a serious head injury. That voice belongs to him, sounds like he is in control. A female voice speaks to Nick on speaker, says he has to ensure April's airways are clear, encourages him to keep checking her breathing and be ready to start CPR if she stops.

'She's out for the count, but she's also breathing by herself. I'll keep monitoring her.'

'Don't worry, I'll stay with you until help arrives,' says the ambulance operator. 'You're doing a great job, both of you.'

Cain holds April's hand, tells her not to worry, everything

is going to be OK, they just have to be a little patient and curses himself for his poor pun. He notices his five grand engagement ring is absent from her wedding finger. The thieving bastards must have pinched the symbol of his and April's eternal unconditional love.

When the first paramedics arrive, they apologise for the delay. Travelling around Manchester quickly is an impossibility, even late on a Sunday night/morning. Too many calls, not enough ambulances. The NHS is on its knees after decades of chronic underinvestment by successive Tory and Labour governments, red or blue, they aren't protecting common people anymore. Same wolves, different clothing, the disadvantaged suffer because they never fight back.

'What happened?' asks a paramedic, gently ushering Cain and Nick away from April's prone body, hands fanning thin air.

'Found her unconscious on the bathroom floor,' Nick says. 'She isn't responding to us.'

'You say she banged her head. Where? On the basin? The toilet?'

'A couple of racist thugs knocked her out by the canal,' Cain says.

'Three muggers,' says Nick.

Cain doesn't bother correcting him, the boxer had been drinking all day and night and was probably hard pushed to name the current prime minister, let alone add up. Although he is being harsh and disrespectful, Cain focuses on April and the medical team surrounding her body, waiting for the professionals to make her better.

'You two have better get dressed,' says a female paramedic, pushing them further out of the way to give the medics more room to treat April. She looks concerned. 'Soon as we have stabilised her, we're blue lighting her in.'

Reluctantly Cain leaves the en suite and grabs the first

pair of Levi 501 jeans, white tee and tennis shoes he can find in his section of their massive walk-in wardrobe. He tends to buy lots of the same item if he likes it. Nick isn't so lucky and puts on Cain's sports clobber several sizes too big for him. He looks like a small child dressing up in his dad's clothes for a laugh. At least he doesn't stink like an unwashed Cain, who thanks Nick yet again for saving April's life.

'Kip here for the night. Take what you want. Food. Drink. Money. Clothes. Sleep in one of the guest rooms.'

The ambulance blue-lights April to North Manchester General Hospital's A&E department in Crumpsall. A team of medics are waiting and take over seamlessly from the paramedics. April queue jumps other crews, and her trolley is pushed into an emergency room off the main corridor. A nurse shows Cain into a quiet waiting room away from the busy A&E's main reception area full of walking wounded, introduces herself as staff nurse Frankie Moore.

'Are you the next of kin?'

'We got engaged tonight. Does that count?'

'No. Sorry. Does she have family, children?'

'Yes. A daughter. We've never met. She's never been to Manchester in the two years me and her mum have been together.'

'What's her name?'

'Summer Sands Ord. April was married to famous Hollywood film director and producer Bob Ord. She's their daughter.'

'My dad has probably heard of him. If April cannot make decisions, her next of kin will be required to act on her behalf. Do you have the daughter's contact details?'

Cain enters the four-digit code into April's mobile and scans her contacts until he finds her daughter. He hands the mobile to Frankie who sends the contact info to herself and vanishes.

Ninety minutes later, Frankie is back in the room with a heavyweight sumo wrestler modelling tight green scrubs. Neurosurgeon Raj Ghandi says a CT scan shows a serious blood clot. He has to open-up April's skull to remove it and stop further bleeding and prevent any secondary swelling. Cain thinks it is better news than last time a neurosurgeon spoke to him and his ex-wife to confirm Hannah was brain dead, and she was only breathing because machines operated her lungs and heart.

'Been here before with my daughter, twenty years ago,' Cain says.

'So sorry to hear that,' says Raj.

'A hit and run. They kept her alive long enough to help others live. Somewhere blind people can see a future, a person with a failing heart and lungs can live and breathe and a drunk has a new liver.'

'Better get started,' says Raj. 'The surgery will take time, but it is straightforward without much risk. We should have a good outcome.'

Raj leaves the room without shaking hands, too pre-occupied with the life-saving challenge ahead taking place at three am in the morning. Cain watches him walk away and wonders how he would cope with the pressure of a life and death job, where one mistake could prove fatal. Chuck Bukowski's *Pull a String, A Puppet Moves* poem about fate dictating unwritten futures springs to Cain's mind. Chuck was a professional alcoholic and womaniser, a nihilist with a $4 million estate. Surprising, considering Chuck spent nearly all his dollars on cigarettes, alcohol, and hookers and squandered the rest, thought Cain, filching an old George Best joke to distract himself from the horror show playing out in front of his eyes. Maybe it was all an act to impress middle classes dullards who got their *walk on the wild side* thrills vicariously. Or Chuck was just smart with money, making sure he got paid and laid before metamorphosing into a performing seal flapping his flippers for attention.

Frankie remains in the room, reassuring Cain by stroking his arm, and handing him a packet of Marlboro Lights with four left in it. No wonder men like Cain fell in love with tactile caring nurses who look slightly seedy and scruffy, a bit like April when he'd first met her.

'Raj is a brilliant surgeon. I've spoken to April's daughter. They were already in the UK, special guests at the Edinburgh International Film Festival. They are getting a taxi now. Should take them four or five hours. The police are outside. They want a word about the attack.'

The cops enter the room and Frankie, despite offering to stay to offer Cain support, leaves. Clad in heavy-duty body-armour, ready for a riot, they introduce themselves, PC Charlie Chen and WPC Greta Golding. They start with easy questions, then sucker punch Cain in the kidneys.

'Have you been drinking, Cain?'

'I proposed. She accepted. We were celebrating.'

'How many?'

'Two glasses of Chablis, possibly three. Why the interest? You won't catch our muggers asking about my drinking habits.'

'We approach all serious assaults with an open mind.'

'You should be chasing a psychopath wearing a black balaclava and sporting a Swastika tattoo. Him and his mate pinched a five grand engagement ring and threw a prestigious award at me in the canal, almost killed me.'

'We've already alerted patrols in the area,' says WPC Golding. 'Did you know two-thirds of women are murdered by a partner or a former partner? How come your knuckles are grazed?'

'Climbing out of a bloody dirty canal. I am the victim, not the criminal here. I didn't hit her.'

'If she dies this could be a murder investigated by detectives twice as bright as us.'

'That wouldn't be difficult,' Cain says.

'We follow every possible line of enquiry. Sorry,' the male uniform says, ignoring Cain's sarcasm.

'I was violently pushed into the canal. April was punched and knocked down by two thugs. A homeless man rescued us. We were wet and cold and stank. We went to our apartment to warm up, shower and wash our clothes. I found April unconscious in the bathroom. That's it,' says Cain.

'This isn't a bizarre sex game that went wrong. A paramedic says all three of you were stark naked?'

Cain doesn't respond to the WPC, thinks if she is after salacious locker room gossip, she can go fuck herself.

'Any more sensible questions? I think the previous one is below your pay grade.'

<h1 style="text-align:center">Five</h1>

Four in the morning, alone in the relatives' room. The cops long-gone, the love of Cain's life is having her skull prised open like a can of baked beans. For two hours he searches April's mobile looking for messages or threads to explain an attack. Nothing stands out. There are lots of new messages congratulating her, and him, on the award and their surprise engagement. April is a popular woman in Manchester. Even Lucy Button wants to make amends and texts his fiancée an apology, 'sorry about tonight, hope you are OK and not hurting too much. We'll have another session on the house and talk about it'. Historic emails and social media threads were about the restaurant business or their busy social lives, visits to the theatre and concerts, charity events for hospices and cancer research, and saving the sick, who were priced out of healthcare options, and marketing promotions and food and drink suppliers' jollies. Lots of messages from Shelley North, her London literary agent responsible for her cooking books, and Fiona Duffin, who also manages April's TV career from the country's capital. Judging from their communications, they were busy dreaming up plans for the next three years when the cold reality is April might have a couple of hours left on the clock.

Drawing a blank and too exhausted to think, Cain distracts himself by playing computer backgammon on April's mobile. He cheats because the app is flawed. If he doesn't like the way the dice fall, he 'undoes' the throw and rolls them again until he has a combination that works for him. If only life was the same, replaying actions and words until you liked the result.

In between rigged games, he rings Vince. Cain leaves another voicemail message with added detail, 'April having brain surgery. Mugged by a thug with a Swastika tattoo. Engagement ring stolen. A homeless ex-boxer called Nick Forti helped us out. Staying at mine overnight. Can we offer him any security work?'

After a few more backgammon games, Cain leaves a message with Cody James, Red Manifesto's general manager, says April is having an emergency operation for a head injury. The restaurant should stay closed until further notice. Tells her to let the staff know and give them a personal guarantee everyone will be paid. Bends her ear about a job for Nick and says he would call her again as soon as he has an update.

Cain posts on the Red Manifesto's social media platforms and website: 'due to unforeseen circumstances, the Red Manifesto will be shut until further notice. Check social media for updates. We apologise for any inconvenience'.

He feels better distracting himself from a life and death battle in a theatre he cannot not influence, although he refuses to offer a prayer to the Big Guy upstairs to save her after he let him down with Hannah. Not that God was ignoring him, he simply doesn't exist. There is no evidence that would ever stand up in a court room and anyone who believes in him, Jesus and the holy spirit turning water into wine was delusional.

Thankfully, there is another Big Guy real enough to do some listening and intervening. Cain accesses his cloud, finds Len Harvey's number and keys it into April's mobile. He dials the number and leaves a voicemail, 'Len, it's Cain Bell. Remember me? A little bird flew over a field and just told me Ted Blake wasn't the driver who killed Hannah Bell. Is it true? Give me a call mate when you pick this up. Speak soon'.

Cain wonders how long before Harvey responds. He'd last seen him the day before he left Manchester, a goodbye pint or two in the Ostrich in Prestwich. One lass flashed her boobs, and another couple duetted on a karaoke version of Meat Loaf's *Paradise by the Dashboard Light* with as much energy as drunken slugs racing to eat a wet lettuce. Len and Cain followed Si and Jay with a boozy rendition of the Clash's *Should I Stay or Should I Go*. When they said goodnight, Harvey told Cain he had made the right decision to leave and that he would see him soon. They'd lost touch with each other. Friendship was like a bar of wet soap, it easily slipped out of your hands.

Six

PC Charlie Chen re-enters Cain's space in the relatives' room at six in the morning, behind him a woman with jet black hair dressed in dark stone jeans and a black tee shirt with a massive red burnished silver cross swinging between temptation valley.

'This is Summer Sands Ord.'

A younger spit of Cain's fiancée breezes into the room. She is tall and bendy like April, but thinner, her face encapsulates childlike innocence, a beauty to launch a thousand ships.

'You must be Cain? Mum never told me anything about an engagement on our weekly catch ups. That's so exciting.'

'I only proposed tonight.'

'Do you mind if we wait here with you? My old man will be here shortly, he's just sorting out the taxi driver and coffees. He didn't want to come with me to MAN-CHEST-ER. Says the city is cursed.'

'Be my guest,' Cain says, with his best welcoming smile. Summer is going to be his stepdaughter in the not distant future when April recovers.

'The nurse says mum had a fall and a bleed on the brain. It's not life threatening, is it? Not like your daughter, Heather. I am so sorry that happened.'

'Very serious,' Cain says and decides not to correct her misnaming Hannah or ask how she knows, although obviously April told her. 'You were right to come down.'

'We should pray for my mum. Feel the full force of the IRA,' she says, taking an expensive leather-bound gold-embossed bible the size of a house brick from her shoulder bag and waving it at Cain.

'IRA?'

'The International Redemption Agency. We are a global faith-based charity helping the vulnerable overcome adversity across the globe. The bible is my gospel, my truth, my guide.'

'Do you have to wear military uniforms like the Salvation Army, the Krishnas and the Sacred Bleeding Hearts of Jesus?' asks Cain, the latter cult from a Rolling Stones' *Far Away Eyes* lyric, Mick and Keef's hilarious country parody of evangelical Americans.

'A leather bible, a silver cross and a belief in the power of prayer. Never heard of the Bleeding Hearts.'

'There's a lot of them around,' says Cain, deciding not to explain his joke, she might not understand his sense of humour as an American. He plays it straight. 'Evangelical Christians. Met a few when I worked in Europe. They take the Bible literally. Is that you?'

'Yes, you may sneer, but God forgives your lack of faith and welcome you into his arms.'

Summer smiles a huge cheesecake grin and clasps her hands, opens her dark brown eyes wide, raises her head and prays.

Oh Holy Spirit, please come amongst us like a dove
Shield and protect now the one that I love.
Cover April's bloody wounds with your grace feathered wings,
Shield April from sorrow, breathe hope from within.
Tend with your goodness the pain that April bears
Heal now April's injuries with miracle care.
Carry April high far above till they see
Your rainbow of promise, real hope lies ahead.
I love April so dearly, so help me to be all that you,
Jesus, would give out his love through me.
Help us free April from adversity.
Like Heather is by your side, forever and ever.

Amen

'Amen,' Cain mumbles with as much postmodern irony he can muster when she finishes sending her message to her God. Does she get special access because she belongs to a religious sect as scary as the Salvation Army, the Hare Krishnas, Scientologists, Christadelphians, and his made-up Sacred Bleeding Heart of Jesus? Why give the bible any credibility beyond it being a subjective anthology penned by witnesses who were often centuries away from the birth, life, death and resurrection of Jesus Christ? Unlike nostalgia rock acts, God & Co never embarked on anniversary tours dispensing free wine, fish, bread and healing the lame and the blind. There is a good reason, none of the miracles happened as reported, they were lost in translation.

'We've raced down from Edinburgh. Didn't have time to book a hotel.'

'You're welcome to stay with us,' Cain says. 'Long as you like.'

'You're too kind. What happened?' asks Summer.

Before Cain has a chance to respond the door opens again and he recognises Bob Ord carrying coffees on a cardboard tray. The Manchester film legend is dressed in a beige suit, flower power shirt and purple boots, a good two decades older than April.

'Bloody Manchester, still grim and miserable.'

Bob hasn't lost his Mancunian accent, despite living in the USA. Story goes he was an ordinary bloke with a wife and two kids, worked in print and was a Labour councillor with Parliamentary ambitions, until he discovered flogging snide posters was more lucrative than protecting society's vulnerable. He used his poster profits to fund drugs and music videos, ditching his first family and his politics. Met April and hit the jackpot with his movie *All Down the Line*, a dark comedy about the drug-addled creation of the Rolling Stones' epic *Exile on Main Street*. Transported Madchester's good, bad and ugly to France for six weeks of summer mayhem.

'Pleased to meet you, Bob. My name's Cain Bell. I am April's...'

'...latest toy boy.'

'...fiancé. We got engaged tonight.'

'I am joking about the age difference. We have eighteen years between us. What happened?'

Cain resists the urge to misunderstand Bob's question and talk about the wedding proposal. There is a cut-off point where black comedy in tragic circumstances becomes oafish and this is one of them. He plays it straight again and gives them edited highlights minus Ted Blake. Summer clutches her silver cross so tight to her chest Cain thinks she might pop a breast. Bob clasps his coffee like a priest offering worshippers the blood of Jesus Christ.

At the end of Cain's mugging monologue, Bob tips the contents of a hip flask into his coffee. The smell of rum wafts in Cain's direction and reminds him of drunken JW Johnsons nights, the late great Tim Bacon's place on Deansgate that revolutionised Manchester's bar culture. Without Aussie Tim there was no Red Manifesto or any other trendy hospitality outlets with wacky names run by bearded hipsters of both sexes.

'Is she going to be OK?' asks Summer.

'She could have permanent brain damage,' Cain says.

'She's a survivor. She's faced worse. Much worse,' replies Bob.

'What's worse than almost dying?'

'If she hasn't told you, I am not telling,' says Bob, as he sips his Jamaican coffee and checks his watch. When Summer leaves to go to the loo, Bob sidles over to Cain, reeking of sweet perfume, spicy rum and old age.

'Between you and me, no need to involve the police or involve Summer. An old friend owes me and can deliver his own street justice.'

'My head of security will sort it out.'

'Who?'

'Vince Crane.'

'Big Vince. Is he still around? We worked on *All Down the Line.*'

'You know Vince?'

'I knew everyone who is anyone in Manchester,' says Bob. 'He was a sparks on the *Line.*'

'Like Ted Blake? April mentioned him tonight out of the blue.'

There is no spontaneous reaction to Blake's name and Cain doesn't expand on what April said about him. Cain studies Bob up close and notices a livid scar on his neck. It looks nasty, an operation or an attack. Not his place to ask.

'Does Ted work for you too as well as Vince? Good to catch up with them both. To be honest, he is more April's friend, did some driving for her in France. He might have introduced me to an investor,' says Bob.

'Who?' Cain asks, noting Bob talks about Ted in the present tense, a clever deception if he knows about the fake confession.

'A long time ago and my memory is poor. Talking about driving, I am going straight back in the taxi to the Edinburgh film festival. Keep an eye on Summer for me, make sure she doesn't get too involved with the local International Redemption Agency. She'll give you my mobile number for the names of your attackers. My friend will do the rest. If you need any help running the Red Manifesto shout.'

'The business runs itself. April runs a very fiscally tight ship,' says Cain.

'She has a brilliant mentor.'

'Intuitive systems triggered by key performance indicators and red-light alarms.'

'Where does she keep her records and documents?'

'In a safe in our apartment.'

'Do you have the combination?'

'Yes but never needed to use it, her privacy zone.'

'Exactly. Never trespass in a woman's garden.'

The film producer is back in his chair when his daughter returns with Raj and Frankie. Are they here to deliver good or bad news? Cain cannot tell from their poker-faces. Death is not a stranger to them; people kick the bucket all the time in hospitals. Just a number's game where they win most but lose too many. The million-dollar question for them all: what is April's fate?

Seven

Raj introduces himself to Bob and Summer, invites everyone to sit down, suggests in a small circle, so he doesn't have to raise his voice too loud and upset others. Although he exudes calmness, the bags under his eyes tell a different story.

'We've stopped the bleeding and lowered her body temperature to thirty-four degrees Celsius while her brain is inflamed, similar to cooling a car engine down.'

'Is she fucked?' asks Bob. 'She's not going to be a vegetable like Michael Schumacher?'

Cain grimaces at April's former husband's insensitivity. Raj doesn't flinch, probably immune to traumatised relatives unable to cope with unexpected trauma.

'Every patient is unique.'

'Is she in pain?' Cain asks.

'No, she's in a medically induced coma,' replies Raj.

'What happens after?' asks Summer, clutching her cross

so hard her knuckles are white.

'A slow recovery begins, an inch at a time.'

'Mum's not going to die?'

'There's no electrical brain activity, but that's normal with her medication. Go home and freshen up,' says Raj. 'If the situation changes, we'll contact you immediately.'

'Who decides to switch the machine off?' asks Bob.

'We're not at that stage and won't be until the sedation drugs wear off.'

'Summer will make the decision, with my help and advice. Officially we're still married, unless she divorced me without letting on, but we're not really connected spiritually anymore, just financially,' says Bob.

'Can I see April?' Cain asks, unaware Bob and April are still married with financial ties. When was she going to drop those bombshells on him?

'Follow me,' says Frankie. 'Raj has another emergency patient to see.'

They tip-toe nervously into the ICU unit. Frankie leads them to the bed. Cain thinks April is beautiful, despite the wires monitoring her.

'Would you mind if I have a few minutes, alone?' Cain asks.

'We'll wait for you outside the front of the hospital with the taxi,' says Bob. 'Don't be too long. I might be gone.'

Alone, Cain sits down, holds her cold hands and strokes them slowly, more for his own of peace of mind than hers.

Cain tells April she has to pull through this crisis and never to leave him by himself. He is at a loss for anything to say. He thinks about describing their perfect wedding once she has divorced Bob, however long that takes. He pictures a civil ceremony in Manchester Art Gallery, taking their vows in the English & French impressionist's gallery. The reception hosted in the Castlefield Viaduct garden overlooking the basin and the city centre. He is a trustee on the viaduct project and heads the comms for the project. He has a list of a hundred and twenty friends to share their special day. He'll add Summer to the list, now he's met April's daughter. He'll invite Bob, if he promises to behave himself, stops acting like a big shot and gives April a quick divorce. The honeymoon is going to be a secret because he wasn't sure April would say yes. It would be expensive, classy and exclusive, somewhere overlooking the Med, a luxury island far away from other tourists.

Cain listens to the hum of ICU machines keeping dead people artificially alive while consultants debate pulling the plug. The nurses keep a respectful distance while he whispers to the most talented and beautiful woman in the world who has betrayed his absolute trust in her. Cain really wants to interrogate her about Ted Blake, shake her awake and demand answers. Is her attack linked to Ted Blake or was it pure co-incidence, rat boys robbing tourists in the big city? Who else knows about Ted Blake and his false confession? Is it an open secret? There are too many questions, never enough answers, just panic, confusion and a justice by-pass. The more he thinks about April and her lies, the angrier he feels, his blood pressure sky high. He must leave before he spontaneously combusts and all that is left of his body is hot ashes and burning-embers on a melting orange plastic chair.

Cain pretends to kiss her but never touches her skin. He departs wounded and hurting, words left unspoken, his anger an unlinked boil. He pauses in a corridor to compose himself, waits for the red mist to disperse and his blood pressure to fall. He sits on a chair and stares at white walls plastered with posters praising hospital staff. Happy faces smile at him. A busy bee wants him to colour him, or her, in and send the finished artwork to the marketing department. Cain can win a hundred quid's worth of M&S vouchers. A poster says, 'an ounce of prevention is worth a pound of cure'. Another encourages patients to, 'trust me, I'm way better than your internet search'. Very true, the internet is a cesspit attracting lowest common denominator thinking and will only get worse.

A tall woman in her mid-forties approaches and sits down next to him. She looks vaguely familiar, but Cain cannot give the face a name. She knows who he is, opens and flicks an ID wallet so he knows who she is too.

'Hello Cain, I am Rita Mann. A friend of April's through her book club. I am a detective with the Greater Manchester police, visiting my sister. Heard about April from the uniforms who interviewed you. Can I have a quick word, off the record?'

'Sure.'

'How is she doing?'

Cain says April's operation has stopped the bleed on her brain and her surgeon has placed her in an induced coma. When she wakes up, she will tell everyone what happened.

'You're not the only couple to have been mugged in Castlefield last night. The two officers who interviewed you took statements from two young white males who claim they were attacked on the same canal pathway as you, a short black man, tall white man, one woman,' says Rita.

'One of them have a Swastika tattoo?'

'You mean Lucas Bone?'

'I didn't get his name. We weren't formally introduced. My attacker was sporting a balaclava and a Nazi logo.'

Without responding to Cain's witticism, Rita flashes a smart phone in front of his eyes. Shows him an image of a handsome young man whose eyes look familiar. She swipes the screen, and another face appears, also familiar, although he's never met or seen him in person before.

'Number one is Lucas before the Nazi hate/hero worship

tattoo and number two is Ryan, Billy McGinty's only son. They are like Siamese twins. They are currently camped out in A&E.' Rita glances again at Cain's grazed knuckles. 'I hope you've done nothing stupid?'

'Like clambering out of the canal before I died of hypothermia? Do I look capable of beating up two young men? Anyway, why are you telling me this?' Cain asks, suspicious about her unofficial approach.

'Off the record, firstly, to keep everyone safe from organised crime. Second, to specifically protect you and April from Billy McGinty. Do you know how you've upset him?'

'Ask him, you're the detective,' says Cain, trying not to sound too flippant.

'It's no laughing matter, Cain. Lucas and Ryan have already told our officers they were mugged same time and place as you,' she says.

'That's a lie.'

'Grow up. A good defence lawyer will claim April banged her head when she fell in the bathroom and that she was never knocked unconscious on the canal path,' says Rita. 'Her intracranial haemorrhage is a simple accident.'

'She was out cold on the cobbles because they attacked her.'

'Your word against theirs.'

'What do I do?'

'Focus on April's recovery,' says Rita. 'Don't let Vince Crane start a bloody war. Keep me informed about anymore threats but leave the policing to us.'

'Like when my daughter was killed twenty years ago?'

'Didn't God take care of Ted Blake?'

Cain snorts at Rita's comment, the famous four is now a secretive six if April and Rita knew about Ted Blake. Who else shares a very public secret and are they all laughing at him? Time to find out and stop perpetuating a worthless macho code of honour.

'According to April, Ted Blake never killed my daughter.'

'If you want to make an official statement, we can go on the record anytime you want, but it all happened a long time ago.'

'How come Len Harvey told you about Blake's confession and no action was taken?' asks Cain.

'It was common knowledge amongst all detectives working in serious crimes, including junior me fresh out of university on a fast forward police graduate scheme. Simple answer, there was no evidence and no time to prosecute before God extracted his own revenge.'

'Do you really believe that?'

'God's revenge? Just a saying. Call it poetic justice, I don't care, I am agnostic. Blake did it, no matter what anyone says. Why would Len and Blake lie?'

'How many other people knew?'

'Dozens,' says Rita. 'It's an open case in theory that is closed in reality. Nobody's been looking for the driver once cancer finished him.'

'No wonder people don't trust the police.'

'That's unfair,' she says. 'I took an oath to serve the Queen with fairness, integrity, diligence and impartiality. Nothing's changed. Unofficially, I believe Ted Blake's confession.'

Cain snorts again, louder this time. Does she really believe what she said? Everybody knows, but nobody ever discusses Hannah's murder. Cain is just as culpable. In the immediate aftermath, he only spoke about Hannah's death to his soon-to-be ex-wife, Mandy, his best mate, Matt Stark, shrink Lucy Button and big Len Harvey.

'I need more than that. You need to prove I can trust you,' says Cain.

'How do I do that?' asks Rita.

'Show me all the police files for Hannah Bell,' says Cain, impressed that she has kept her calm despite his unnecessary provocation, presumably she's been offered and called a lot worse. Goes with the territory.

'Hell might freeze over first before I put my career and pension at risk.'

'So it is a no? You're not really interested in catching the bad guys, by hook or by crook?'

'It's very lonely on the top of the mountain taking the higher moral ground, Cain. I hope April recovers quickly.'

Has Rita passed or failed the integrity test? Who knows? She isn't in the mood for any further discussions. Simply nods and walks away, shaking her head ruefully. Cain smiles at the brilliant post-modern irony of his request, asking her to prove her honesty to him with her dishonesty to her employer.

Eight

Cain gives Rita a head start and follows her from a distance as she marches towards the exit signs and the upper car park of the old sprawling Victorian site. When she steps outside, he watches from a window on a staircase as she walks straight to her black Audi A4, gets in and drives off alone, her message delivered on behalf of the Greater Manchester police, Len Harvey, Billy McGinty, or whoever else pulls her strings.

Cain backtracks and follows the directions towards the hospital entrance. Bob and Summer are chuffing away on their tabs in the disabled car park across the road from the entrance to the hospital. The two of them look like thin bendy extras, escapees from a Lowry painting. The rent collecting artist is synonymous with the doom and gloom of Salford and Manchester's real industrial heritage. Next to them is another Lowry refugee, a pink woman dressed in bright pink jeans, pink leather jacket and a pink beanie.

All three of them glance at Cain as he walks towards them. The pink lady leaves Bob and Summer and heads in his direction, intercepting Cain before he crosses the road.

'You must be Cain Bell. Congratulations. Saw all those social media posts last night announcing your engagement to April at the Manifesto. Just bumped into Bob and Summer. They told me the dreadful news about April's accident. My son is in A&E with his best mate, lovely lad called Lucas, both mugged last night, cuts and bruises and a loss of face. I am just collecting Ryan and Lucas. Save on the taxi.'

'Who are you?'

'Sorry. I am Violet. Violet McGinty. An old friend of April's. Our children are the same age, born within days of each other. How is she doing? It's not that serious, is it?'

'Dancing on the edge of a very sharp Japanese cooking knife,' Cain says, an image conjures up memories of April in a bar in Norway moving to music only she heard.

Violet looks sombre, despite her pink varnished nails, beaded hair extensions, excessive bling and black ink tattoos, and an exposed washboard midriff, similar to April's caesarean scarred podgier belly.

'Who would have thought your home could be a potential death trap? Did she bang her head on the bath, toilet or the sink?'

'Neither. She was mugged in Castlefield,' Cain says.

'Just like Ryan and Lucas. That part of town is a real health hazard for tourists.'

'Any ideas who mugged your son and his friend?'

'No. A black and white mixed-race attack, according to Ryan. One tall, one short. Probably illegal immigrants wanting a free ride. To be honest, nowhere is safe anymore.'

'They are asylum seekers,' Cain says.

She smiles again and glances at his damaged knuckles.

'That's a bit woke for me, Cain. What have you told the police about your attack?'

'Only what I saw. One of them has a Swastika tattoo on his right cheek.'

'Did he? Like this?'

She reaches up to Cain's face and draws an outline of a Nazi logo the size of two-pound coin on his cheek. He doesn't flinch or try to stop her run her false nail gently over his skin. Her breath smells of cigarettes, peppermints and gin.

'I am not scared of your husband,' Cain says.

'What are you talking about?' asks Violet. 'We're pussycats, virtually semi-retired. Billy spends all his time playing country songs and strumming his acoustic guitar, a bloody Martin. Wants to write his memoirs, except he has a big problem.'

'Why did you attack us?' asks Cain, unwilling to discuss the creative writing ambitions of Manchester's most notorious gangster.

'We didn't,' she replies and pulls a sad face and toys with her hair extensions like a schoolgirl, her eyes filling up again like she could cry on demand. 'As I said, me and April are friends. Why would we want to hurt her? And you? April is the kindest, most loving person I've ever met in my entire life. We are like sisters.'

'She's never mentioned you since I've known her. Why's that?' Cain asks.

'Grief intervened, the loss of her stillborn son in France was too much,' says Violet. Tears flow down her face, and she wipes them away and smudges her mascara. 'I was in France with her. We gave birth within 48 hours of each other. Me first and then her, both of us caesareans. She had hers because she was carrying twins and there was a worry one of them wasn't moving. One kicked on one side, but not on the other. Me, I had an umbilical cord prolapse. They were worried Ryan may not get enough oxygen.'

'When was this?'

'Summer of '97. Bob was shooting *All Down the Line* and it was all hands to the pump because Bob was on a tight budget. We were extras and crew. Pregnancy fitted with the movie's hippy vibe. The film was almost finished when we both gave birth, her on 27 August and me on the 28th. Like I said, neither of us planned caesareans. We had to wait while we recuperated before we went home.'

'She never told me the detail,' Cain says. 'Just that she had a stillborn, a boy called Eric. That's all. Nothing else. Never discussed it. Like I never discussed the death of my daughter. We're still grieving.'

'Sorry for your loss. Why would anyone want to talk about a stillborn child? Look, I've got to dash. Ryan and Lucas are waiting. Call me. Anything I can do to help April, just ask,' says Violet, handing Cain a pink business card. The address is a farm in Sinister between Middleton and Prestwich in North Manchester. He slips the card into the back pocket of his jeans.

'They stole a five grand engagement ring. I'd like it back. My mobile is lying on the bottom of the canal and some serious clobber ruined. Comp for that too. Most importantly I want April restored to full health, but you can't do that. And an apology.'

'I would want one too if I is you. Are you using her mobile?'

'What's it to you?'

'A contact number. I'll get Billy to ask around, see if anyone is trying to flog an engagement ring on the cheap. You can give it back to April when she wakes up.'

'And if she doesn't?'

'I'll catch up with her in heaven one day.'

'Or hell? You could say hello to dead Ted Blake? He went

straight to hell after killing my daughter in a black golf! Except it wasn't him. Fake news.'

'Sorry to hear about your daughter. Why are you mentioning Ted? Not heard his name for years.'

She is a good actress, Cain gives her that for nothing. Like Bob she controls her emotions, except the exaggerated pulse on her neck explodes twice as she assimilates his words. A nervous red rash spreads around her neck and chest, her forehead glistens with a thin veneer of sweat.

Guilty.

'You anything to tell me about Ted?' Cain asks.

'Get a life Cain, it is a long time ago and you shouldn't speak evil of the dead. Not nice.'

'Cough up about Ted and my daughter and Sunday's attack never happened.'

'I'll keep your petulance from Billy, he's more black and white than me.'

She wipes the coy schoolgirl innocence from her face and stares Cain down hard as nails, letting her unambiguous threat sink in. She changes tack from her earlier friendlier self. After three or four beats she goes, their chat over.

Cain blinks and makes his way across the road to Bob and Summer, lights a cigarette and feels the nicotine hit calm him. They look sheepish once he rejoins them, as if they are watching gay porn in a public place.

'How do you know Violet McGinty?'

'An old friend of a friend when me and April first got together. Her son's been mugged. She's collecting him from casualty,' says Bob.

'So she says. Thought you were going back to Scotland.'

'Change of plan,' says Bob. 'I can do it next year.'

'Why the change of heart?'

'My wife and daughter need me more. You might need some help running the Red Manifesto now you're missing

April's brains and experience. As a major shareholder with a track record of delivering profits, I can add my financial clout and contacts to your business.'

'How altruistic.'

'No need to be sarcastic.'

'Will she be bringing her son back this way?' Cain asks Bob, unsure how he will react to seeing his muggers in the flesh.

'That's her car,' says Bob, nodding at a black Range Rover. 'And this is my — our — taxi.'

'We should scoot before she comes back with our attackers,' says Cain, thinking Bob staying because he's big mates of the McGintys, yet another April secret. How many more are hidden up her sleeves?

Nine

Twenty minutes later Cain, Bob and Summer are in the lift to his and April's skyscraper apartment. Cain hopes Nick Forti isn't unconscious in a pool of piss after polishing off a month's supply of Oliver's cider. That is uncool and an abuse of their hospitality. When they enter the apartment, they hear loud grunting. Cain thinks Nick is either lifting heavy weights, masturbating, or shagging his cleaner, Ulrike Bonn. If it is the latter, Nick has at least waited until she tidied up before giving her one. The apartment looks immaculate, washed clothes neatly folded, cups and glasses washed, bottles ready to be recycled.

'Nick, it's Cain,' he shouts, remembering Ulrike comes on Wednesdays and Fridays. She is at university the other days studying fine art.

A topless Nick pops his head out of the gym, soaked in sweat and dressed in baggy shorts.

'How is April?'

Cain updates him quickly. Cain introduces Nick to Summer and Bob.

'We've met before,' says Bob. 'Won a few quid on him. Lost a whole lot more. You're looking in good shape, Nick.'

'Would like to say the same about you. Life's been too good, Bob.'

Cain laughs at Nick's wit and turns a guffaw into a gruff cough to clear the frog in his throat when he sees Bob's reaction, no point ruffling his feathers for no reason.

'Stunning views,' Summer says, as she stares out over Cheshire, Merseyside and Wales. 'You and mum must have been very happy here.'

'We were. Still might be,' Cain says, without much conviction.

'What's your internet password?' asks Bob.

Cain tells him where to find it on the back of the router in the sitting room overlooking the city centre.

'I can't cook like April, but even I cannot mess up scrambled eggs and marinated smoked salmon.'

'Let me do it. I can earn my keep,' says Nick.

'Is he staying?' asks Bob. 'There are only three bedrooms.'

'The sofa or the floor in the gym is fine with me,' says Nick. 'I slept on the sofa last night. Not the bed.'

'Let's eat, I'll prep breakfast quickly.' Cain goes to the fridge, brings out the ingredients and tells his guests how April loves to experiment with recipes at home, calls them her tiny little creations. Films herself when she cooks new things and sends videos to her agents Shelley and Fiona for professional feedback, but he is the one who sees and eats them first. 'We were an equal partnership, and we loved each other unconditionally. There are two guest bedrooms. They have en suites. Beds are made up just in case friends want to crash. We should eat and grab an hour and then go back in.

It's been exhausting and terrifying in equal measure.'

They agree and after scoffing breakfast double quick time Cain goes into the master bedroom for a sixty-minute catnap. He drifts in and out of consciousness. Imagines April and himself walking hand in hand on a deserted beach in Farsund, Norway, overlooking the North Sea, talking food, music, literature and films and the places they frequented in Manchester when they were young, innocent and undamaged by personal tragedy.

When Cain wakes, he expects April to be with him, same as he does with Hannah, stirring each morning for twenty years, anticipating her shouting out to her mum or him in that excited voice that greeted everyday as if it was Christmas.

For a fraction of a split second, April is there, the most beautiful woman in the world, Cain's fiancée. He reaches out across the empty bed, not knowing if he will ever sleep with her again. And then he remembers what she said about Ted Blake and their tainted love is contaminated, their trust irrevocably broken.

Cain glances at the Alexa Echo by the side of his bed. He has hardly blinked, and it is already 10.45am. April's mobile rings, no Caller ID. Cain reaches across, picks up the handset and expects her London agents to be on the phone demanding news about their cash-cow client. How did they find out so quickly?

'Is that April, April Sands?'

'No, who's calling.'

'I recognise those sexy dulcet tones. Hi Cain, it's Nancy Hood. What's this I hear about bizarre sex games getting out of hand — you, April Sands, the Asian celebrity TV chef, and a punch-drunk black boxing champ? Want to tell me all about your fuck-buddy love triangle?'

'Hi Nancy, nice to hear from you,' Cain says.

'Ditto.'

Cain pictures her, a former hotshot regional journalist, now a red-eyed pisspot peddling online click-bait bullshit. She was once an untouchable with eyes only for editors to give her a quick bunk up the journalistic greasy pole.

'We're speaking off the record, aren't we?'

'Sure. My sources say you two regularly pick up the homeless for threesomes.'

'Your sources are mistaken,' Cain says, thinking Nancy has just called April an Asian chef. She must be in a permanent state of racist inebriation.

'Anything you'd like to say on the record?'

'No story here, Nancy. April is in intensive care after brain surgery, but that's private and off the record. Me and her, still off the record, were mugged by a couple of opportunist thieves. If you want a story, write about the serial killer responsible for 70 canal deaths in the city over two decades.'

'That's fiction, exploitation TV. I want real stories with legs.'

'Who is your source again?' Cain asks.

'A good journalist never reveals her sources?'

'But what about bad ones like me and you?'

'Still your self-deprecating self. Shall we go on the record? I am going to write something.'

'Not while she's fighting for her life.'

'I repeat, do you regularly pick up homeless men for bedroom romps?'

'Don't be crazy.'

'Nick 'Thor' Forti is the boxer's name I've been given, a pugilist turned rent boy?'

'April is really ill,' he says, wondering who has contacted her. The two uniforms who interviewed him? Rita Mann? Hospital or ambulance staff? How does she know about Nick, unless he's the source?

'Cut the crap, Cain. I'll write you're a sulky 'no comment' from behind a closed door in a giant penthouse owned by April.'

'Nancy, don't...'

The line goes dead before Cain can warn her about the Billy 'Mad Dog' McGinty link. She would have spiked the story faster than she could knock back a snakebite and whiskey chaser in a blob shop back in the day when drunken hedonism wasn't a newsroom sin.

Cain calls his drinking buddy and the local daily newspaper crime reporter, Matt Stark, to share his dreadful news. Like everyone else whoever suffered a tragedy, he needs good friends around him in a crisis. Matt is the best, and, unlike Vince Crane and Len Harvey, answers second ring.

'Hey Cain, a great night last night. You been to bed yet? And the answer is yes to the best man gig, if I am not jumping the gun!'

'April's critically ill. She's just had brain surgery and is in an induced coma.'

'What the fuck?' asks Matt. 'How is she?'

'Off the record, possibly knocking on heaven's door,' Cain says and tells him the story.

'Fucking hell, Cain.'

Matt's voice changes when Cain mentions Lucas Bone and Ryan McGinty and meeting Violet McGinty at the hospital.

'What's Billy 'Mad Dog' McGinty really like behind the anecdotes and mythology?'

'I've been a crime reporter for twenty-five years, Cain. Most gangsters love us glamming them up. They are dead friendly, trying to impress us with their exaggerated stories wanting our approval. McGinty doesn't care about anything. Does read the stories we write about him. Never reads them back to us. Not even the headlines. Avoid him and his XL Bully dogs. No point ending up as dog food or fish bait in the North Sea.'

'Why are we on their radar?' Cain asks.

'Who knows. Get off it as fast you can. You've heard the story about Jimmy Bone?'

'No,' lies Cain. 'Give me your version.'

'Jimmy was his best mate but disappeared when they fell out over a car deal. One of them claimed it was a gift. The other says cash was due. A thousand quid. They were due to have a dust up in a squash court at a sports club in Middleton. Legend has it King Billy let his dogs do the fighting for him. Jimmy's not the only notch on his bedpost. Make sure you're not the next, mate! This is not something we can laugh off over a couple of pints.'

'What do we do?'

'Pray it's a case of mistaken identity or negotiate a truce.'

'Could I reason with Violet? She gave me her business card?'

'Appearances are deceptive. She looks like a Saturday Night Girl ready to drop her knickers for a free Pina Colada and a packet of prawn cocktail crisps. She's playing mind games with you. She is as ruthless as him, the brains behind his money. I'll put out a few feelers for you, but I cannot promise anything,' says Matt, echoing what he said almost word for word when Hannah was killed. Matt is a good investigative reporter, but even he found nothing, despite his numerous underworld contacts. 'What about covering the story in the paper? Now you've told me. It's going to be viral on socials soon.'

'Wait until the police let you know about the incident at their daily press calls. When you get the story officially, we're devastated by the mugging and her family, including her fiancé Cain Bell, former husband Bob Ord and daughter

Summer Sands Ord. They are united by her bedside. The family would like to thank the emergency services for saving her life. The restaurant was closed until further notice. The family asked everyone to respect their privacy during these trying times. Call me a spokesman for the restaurant. If you use my name, I'll get abused on social media by conspiracy theorists claiming I did her for the insurance or that she is having an affair with Joy Division's Ian Curtis or John Lennon.'

'OK boss, you sound very authoritative, now you're an entrepreneur,' says Matt.

'One more thing. Nancy Hood rang me. She's after sex click-bait. Can you give her a call? Warn her off-the-record about the possible McGinty family's involvement. That should kill her silly story stone dead.'

'Consider it done.'

Cain momentarily thinks about adding the Ted Blake bombshell to the mix but knows Matt might be upset if Cain never told him at the time. Matt would see it as betrayal of their friendship and mates should never retrospectively acknowledge secrets. Fuck him, what about Cain's feelings? What if Matt knows, like every detective in Manchester. Matt has many sources inside the police feeding him tit bits. Cain has been passive for too long; his silence is disrespecting his dead daughter.

'You know when you investigated Hannah's death all those years ago?'

'Yes?'

'Did the name Ted Blake ever crop up as the driver who might have killed Hannah, your goddaughter?'

Cain listens to the pause as he catches his best friend off guard. He hears the cogs working while the crime reporter decides how to answer a very simple but awkward yes or no question. Matt deploys a classic journalistic device to buy himself thinking time.

'How do you mean?'

'You would have told me?'

'Sure,' says Matt, relief seemingly permeating through his voice that Cain's not accusing him of anything.

'Crossed wires, mate, still up for best man when April's on her feet?'

'Job's a good one, Cain. Laters.'

Matt bloody knows, Cain would swear on it. Asking him outright would endanger their friendship and Matt's health if the criminals believed he was a grass.

Cain calls Cody James, Red Manifesto's general manager, who answers with concern in her voice and a frog in her throat. Cain keeps it simple and confirms his previous message about closing until further notice.

'Vince says we should close today out of respect for April but reopen tomorrow. I am sure me and him can manage the business while you two are away. We'll need you to sign off the wages later in the week, but we can run things until she's better. If we close any longer, Vince says the business will struggle. We'll lose all the positive PR of the last two years.'

'When did you speak to Vince?'

'About an hour ago.'

'He's not called me.'

'Says you have enough on your plate.'

'The restaurant stays closed until further notice.'

'Vince says...'

'Forget Vince. I am the boss. Not him.'

Conversation over with Cody, Cain tries Vince and goes to voicemail, yet again. Cain asks him to call urgently. Vince normally replies the instant Cain calls. They have a lot to discuss that can only be done face to face. Has the McGinty family told Vince to ostracise Cain? Although the Red Manifesto pay Vince three grand a week to protect the business and its staff, clearly it is not enough. Vince and Cain are close friends, but they both know there is no point to being the best dressed corpse in the cemetery because he's hacked off Billy McGinty. The writing on Vince's wall is written in large CAPITALS for any idiot to comprehend, 'we doff our caps to the McGinty clan, like they are our very own royal family'. Matt probably faces the same dilemma too, risking his life to help a friend find the truth? That is a huge ask for anyone, unless they are exceptionally brave or stupid — like Nick Forti.

Can Cain swallow that bitter pill to give McGinty a free ride? What choice does he have? Attack Mad Dog with a pea shooter and call him names on social media? Cain's best option is to ask for an impartial meditator like Len Harvey to intervene — once the outsized detective has cleared up the confusion over Ted Blake's false confession — and restore everything back to normal.

Ten

Bob and Summer look very pleased with themselves when Cain walks into the sitting room after his snooze. They are sitting on the same large four-seater leather sofa where Cain and April would snuggle up to watch the telly whenever they have a rare night off from the Manifesto. April is easily bored when she has nothing to do but think. Watching boring TV is usually a good excuse for them to get frisky.

'Where's Nick?'

'Follow the pig noises!'

Cain does, Nick is sleeping off his exertions in the gym. Cain looks in, Nick is curled up on the exercise mat, gently snoring.

'Busy on the phone?' asks Summer, looking up from her bible and toying with her red burnished silver cross, picking her fingernails with the sharp corners. 'We could hear you talking loads.'

'Restaurant business,' Cain replies. 'And catching up with a mate, you need good friends around you in a crisis.'

'We've been busy too,' says Bob, smiling. 'My insurance people have agreed to fund a private clinic in California because we're still married. Soon as April is fit to travel, my health insurers will ensure my wife is seen by the very best brain specialists in the entire universe. Her future medical care is covered even if she stays in a coma or is declared brain dead, the deal for all three of us is that comprehensive. As a last resort we freeze her and wait until the science improves,' says Bob, speaking as if the decision has already been made.

'Hold on, Bob, you're going too fast.'

Maybe Cain is still too groggy from the catnap. Is Bob suggesting stuffing April in the freezer like a loaf of bread or a pint of milk until lunatics figure out how to defrost dead people and bring them back to life like a Netflix horror movie?

'I'll speak slower,' says Bob, making space for Cain to sit next to him as he shares his iPad's screen. 'This is the Emily Frances Head Injury Clinic in Los Angeles. It is the best medical care centre in the world for serious head injuries. I reserved a place for April while you were chatting to your mates. The room is ready and waiting for her whenever we fly her over. Look ...'

'All this within a couple of hours of life-saving brain surgery...?'

'I am pragmatist, old chap. Time waits for no one, and it won't wait for us if we sit here moping, feeling sorry for ourselves. There is more. A very good Hollywood film producer friend of mine needs a new head of corporate PR for his studio. I think you'd be an ideal replacement given your track record as a journalist and as a public relations officer. He agrees you would be a great champion and social conscience for his studios. Hal King's package is very attractive.'

'Why the job offer?'

'So April can make a full recovery at the Emily Frances Head Injury Clinic with you and Summer by her side.'

'Why do all this for me?'

'Not for you, you're the last thing on my mind, if I am being honest. You're her latest toy boy along for the ride and I don't blame you. I am doing this for my daughter so Summer gets closer to her mother. They've not shared too much time together in their lives for one reason or another, probably why Summer's embraced her nutty friends in the International Redemption Agency. Together you will help return April to full health, stay at our house as long as you don't start shagging Summer, she's not part of the deal. My joke. I don't care if you do, just an exchange of fluids, but she hasn't got a grandad complex. I would...if she wasn't my flesh and blood. Another joke, the sort of thing Donald Trump says in the Oval Office and sick people applaud him. Real life is always stranger than fiction. Let me show you the house.'

Bob flicks through another slide show, revealing an equally stunning expensive coastal residence.

'Impressive,' Cain says, unsure if he is truly impressed or just being polite, the house looks like a fantasy film set for the rich and famous.

'Our home has massive oceanfront decks with endless spectacular views where you can enjoy warm California sun, not bloody freezing Manchester despair. And it is all yours and Summer's. We agreed? We can tell the hospital when we visit again?'

Cain doesn't know what to think. Bob's proposition sounds crackpot crazy yet totally sensible, although it is mental to be talking about the future when April's fate hangs in the balance. Another opportunity to run from the scene of the crime, like he did six-months after Hannah's demise.

'I don't know what to say. Generous beyond belief.'

'You'll be free from a bankrupt and incompetent NHS.'

'That easy?'

'You and Summer can be there as early as tomorrow. Or anytime you want. Use our existing tickets. Change my name to yours. We have a deal?'

'What about the Red Manifesto?'

'You'll love the USA, we'll help you sell it. Corporate hospitality businesses will be queuing up outside to buy the place. You'll make your investment back and then some more. We'll all make a good return on our cash.'

'Who is we?'

'Me, April and a few friends.'

'Do I know them?'

'They are sleeping partners. Don't worry about them.'

'I don't.'

'I can handle all the business transactions for you when the time is right. Bread and butter for me. You said all her paperwork is in her safe in your bedroom?'

'Do you want me to open it?'

'No. We've got other things to focus on.'

'What about your earlier proposition?'

'Which one?'

'About beating up the muggers, your friend who administers street justice?'

'Did I suggest that? Must have been pissed, too much North Berwick Rum. Sorry. Life's too short. Probably opportunists looking for unsuspecting tourists. Drug addicts more than likely. Vince can sort them out in his own time.'

'Did you know Billy McGinty as well as his wife Violet? When did you last see him?'

'Not seen Billy since we filmed *All Down the Line* in France. Seeing his wife was a pure fluke, forget them both. Let us concentrate on the present and a bright future. America is a good opportunity for you, April and Summer. There's no rush, but the sooner we get motoring, the better. Shall we go and see how she is doing?'

'Are you OK with this Summer?' Cain asks. 'It's all a bit quick and dramatic?'

She isn't listening, instead clutching the cross tight to her chest, whispering to herself, almost in a trance.

Dear Lord,

Your love for April is as wide as the oceans, as deep as the sea, and as tall as the heavens.
Release the full power of your spirit, let it rise like a mighty wave and come and restore my beloved April's health.
You are the water of life. You are a fresh spring.
You are healing rain to all those when April is in need.
Come, Lord, in our hour of need, show us the way....
Amen.

No need to petition the Lord with prayer, Summer. Cain has an offer of an overseas rebirth, no miracles needed, just deep guilty pockets stuffed with cash. Why is Bob trying to buy Cain off? Was Bob the driver that ran Hannah down? Is that how April knows it wasn't Ted Blake? Bob confessed to her all those years ago and she never told Cain until her conscience forced her to say something when he proposed?

Cain thanks Bob for his kind offer, says he doesn't need to sleep on it because he is one hundred percent for the plan. It is inspiring and he can never find the words to express his gratitude. There is one thing.

'What if she dies before we get to the USA?' asks Cain.

'That's not going to happen.'

'Why?'

'Positivity talks, Cain. PMA all the way. I'm glad I moved to the USA otherwise I'd be a boring bastard like Ken Loach or Mike Leigh relying on public money to make depressing films about poverty porn and emasculated losers. You're not one of them Cain, are you? April wouldn't fall for a jerk off who cries every time he looks in the mirror and sees a spot on the end of his beak?'

'She fell for you once upon a time,' says Cain, 'and you're hardly matching Hemingway or Mailer in the macho stakes, despite the scar on your neck.'

'That was an accident,' says Bob.

'Serious question, if she dies in America, am I cut adrift?'

'No. She'll become one of the 500 ultra rich people frozen in time, ready to be thawed out and become a functioning human again once the science is ready.'

'Are you on the ice-dead list?'

'Me and Walt Disney and Elon Musk,' smiles Bob. 'And Donald Trump in time for his fifth term as a president.'

'Your insurance doesn't cover me?' asks Cain, trying hard not to sound too post-modern ironic, or what others call sarcastic.

'No. Are you important enough to justify the premiums?'

'Hopefully not.'

The two men look at each and decide to call their banter a score draw. Although the cryonics clause appears to be totally crazy and a sign of desperation to get Cain out of the country, they have agreed a healthcare solution. The immediate priority now is to be next to April when she wakes up. Whenever that happens, she needs all her friends around her because she won't have a clue who or where she is. She could wake up in rainy Manchester or open her eyes in sunny California in a few days or decades from now. They would all be there ready and waiting for her to name and shame the killer of Cain's daughter.

Eleven

There is no change at the hospital when they arrive early afternoon, refreshed and rinsed, ready to play the waiting game. They are met by Cathy Moore, the senior ICU sister caring for April. Cathy, a red head with a kind smile, makes them feel at ease with her relaxed manner. Says they have probably met her sister, Frankie, who works in A&E. She says April is still critical and under constant medical supervision in the intensive care unit. While she isn't out of danger, she isn't deteriorating either.

For Cain that is good news compared to Hannah's timeline when it was apparent there were no signs of life. The ventilator kept her breathing while everyone talked transplants. Cain's wife Mandy, a bit like Summer, was convinced miracles happened if she prayed hard enough.

Cain believed in the science and said they must accept Hannah's inevitable fate. If they could help others...they should, it was the humane thing to do. Hannah would have wanted to help others if they'd been able to ask her. She loved animals, had pets of her own, and was a committed environmentalist even at the tender age of eleven, writing stories for school about global warming and climate change and rising sea levels.

There is no point Cain sharing his previous experiences with Summer and Bob. They won't understand. Not yet, while there is hope for April. Only the relatives and friends of dead people taken violently without any warning empathise with the shock and the pain. Cain can bury his deep, but the pain resurfaces when he least expects it. He's lost count of the number of times he's been convinced he's seen Little Miss Red Dress, dozens, if not hundreds, of times. Sometimes he's followed a girl through city streets or country lanes or on sandy beaches, preparing to take her by surprise, say hello, and hug her, until he realises it is just his imagination torturing and teasing him.

Summer asks Cathy a few questions while Bob and Cain watch on. Cathy says April's big moment comes when they wean her off the drugs over the next day or two. April will either emerge from her coma or enter a vegetative state where she is unaware of her surroundings, or anything else. Cathy explains her vegetative state could be permanent, although individuals often progress to a minimally conscious state if she shows any signs of self-awareness or awareness of her environment.

'What about brain death? What's that?' asks Summer.

'If the brain and brainstem aren't functioning when we remove her breathing devices, she is dead. Brain death is irreversible. We're nowhere near that yet, are we?'

'Who makes the actual medical decision to switch the

machine off?' asks Summer. 'I am not qualified. Nor is my dad or Cain.'

'Our team will make a medical assessment and recommendation and then ask you to confirm you're happy with the medical decision. You don't make it in isolation without all the facts or a proper medical assessment.'

Satisfied, Summer asks about transplants if her mum is brain dead. Cain thinks it is a brave question for her, and, for once, doesn't involve a nonsense prayer to her omnipresent God. Cathy explains that the surgical and transplant teams work completely independently of each other to ensure there is never any conflict of interest. If it is appropriate, they will be in touch.

Bob, who has been remarkably passive throughout the discussion, waits for his moment in the sun, puffs out his chest and outlines his plans for April's recovery in the USA at the Emily Frances Head Injury Clinic. He asks Cathy how soon he can connect the relevant people to make things happen. She says she would call somebody to come and talk to him within the hour. She suggests they wait in the quiet room next to ICU or sit with April, as she may be touched by their presence.

'If nothing else it will make you all feel better being so close,' says Cathy.

An hour later, Summer, Bob and Cain sit awkwardly by April's bedside, the father and daughter on one side, the fiancé on the other. Cain holds April's cold right hand while Summer grasps her left. The ICU unit is cold, the machines noisy, the staff busy, voices barely above a whisper. Other relatives gather around their loved ones, half a dozen humans fighting for their lives, playing the numbers game. Some will live, some will die, nobody will ever be the same again.

The three of them spend half an hour in sullen silence staring at April locked in a medically induced coma before

Cathy Moore returns to collect Bob to kick start the practicalities of transporting April lock, stock and barrel across the Atlantic Ocean. Cain thinks the film producer is embarking on a mission impossible to transfer a critically ill comatose patient five thousand miles, but he knows money opens doors that ordinarily stay locked.

After the initial adrenaline rush, the reality of April's situation kicks in. There is nothing an exhausted Cain can say to help ease her pain or distress, so he says nothing and waits for Summer to ask questions or start a conversation. She doesn't. She just clutches her cross deep into her chest, picks her nails, and reads, or whispers, her bible for an hour or so.

Finally, she speaks.

'Did you go through the same thing with Heather?' asks Summer.

'I don't like talking about my daughter,' replies Cain, truthfully, he has not really mentioned her to anyone since returning from his exile to Manchester. 'Still too raw.'

'We should do something to cheer ourselves up, inject some positivity into our veins,' says Summer, delving into her shoulder bag.

'As long as it doesn't involve reading the bible or you praying to God,' says Cain, without thinking what a knob he is being, insulting her religion and bullying her for no reason. Not a good look for a mature man speaking down to a young vulnerable woman, especially when her mother is critically ill.

Summer looks hurt for a second and then smiles and stops searching in her bag. Cain apologises for his insensitivity and tries to make a joke out of it, says he shouldn't mock people because of their religious beliefs just because he is a vocal atheist and a £10 a month humanist, another spontaneous quip he often drops unnecessarily into conversations.

He reluctantly acknowledges the homeless problem in Manchester, and elsewhere in the western world, would be a lot worse without the intervention of charities like the International Redemption Agency whose good deeds are welcome. Cain reaches across with his free hand and invites Summer to hold his, all three of them link in a chain like they are ready to simultaneously pull crackers at Christmas.

'Jesus understands your frustration. Me too, as one of his chosen IRA ambassadors. Why not tell me how you met my mum. You're going to be my stepdad when she recovers and we'll be related by marriage? I know nothing about you, other than what she's told me. We've got plenty of time to tell each other our life stories.'

'Fire away... then you can decide, good guy, bad guy?'

'Good Cain, bad Cain? The Bible says Cain is a rebellious man who rejected God's plan, ignored God's warnings, and received God's judgment,' says Summer and she laughs and tells her comatose mother she is only joking.

'I am not that man,' says Cain.

'How many questions do I get to prove it one way or another?'

'Six should be enough. I don't want to bore you to sleep.'

'When did you first meet my mum?'

A good question, they were both in Manchester in the nineties and visited lots of the same places. They were on nodding terms; him a journalist and she was one of the cultural elite.

'Farsund, on the southern tip of Norway. An international food festival, she was one of the guest speakers. I was based in Oslo and working as a tour guide showing small groups around Scandinavia. I took six Americans brewers and their wives to Farsund for an overnight stay and we ended up drinking in a club after her show. Two things stood out for me. She was the most beautiful women in the world, and she danced alone to music only she could hear. Half cut, I went over and said hello, my name is Cain Bell, I'd love you to cook that Creamy Norwegian Fish Soup for me, she says she'd be honoured, and we gelled immediately. Talked and drank all night long until 3am. Music, books, films, drinking, eating and the joy of being free spirits without any baggage or children or partners. Next morning, when my group was leaving to go to Stavanger for a four-hour hike to the Preikestolen, she joined us. We've been together virtually every day ever since.'

'That's so romantic. How come you lied to each other about your kids?'

'We were chatting to each other like teens, a one-night stand, or a week's fling. Nothing serious at the time. It didn't matter. A week later, we were still together back in Oslo, and she told me about you and Eric, your still-born twin, and I told her about Hannah. Just the headlines. Not the detail. We acknowledged each other's grief and left it at that. To me it felt like a new beginning after all the grief.'

'Hannah. I thought she is called Heather. Why didn't you correct me?'

'No point. You got the H right, which is better than a lot of people. You know, I've never talked in detail about any of this to anybody. You're the first.'

'I am your virgin listener?'

'Something like that, next question?'

'Why did you move back to Manchester when you had a life in Oslo?'

'We talked about our dreams and what we wanted to achieve as we'd both hit our fifties. I'd been living a peripatetic existence since I'd left Manchester. I'd travelled all over Europe, worked in publishing and property in Berlin for four years, ran a coffee shop next to the beach in Nice for five years, lived in Krakow in Poland, and was a tour guide at

Auschwitz, showing groups of Americans and Brits around the extermination camp, reliving Nazi horrors four times a day, five days a week for four years, I spent another four in Dublin doing in-house PR for a well-known brewery and twelve months in Oslo.'

'A tour guide at Auschwitz? Sounds like you're punishing yourself?'

'Perceptive. Is that one of the six questions?'

'No.'

'I'll answer it anyway.'

Cain says it was a mission, keeping the holocaust alive, denying the deniers the opportunity to dismiss the final solution as a conspiracy theory. He'd been in Krakow on a break from France and somebody told him in a bar they were looking for guides. They always were because it was tough retelling the story of the largest mass murder in a single location in human history day after day. More people died at Auschwitz than at any other Nazi concentration camp and probably than at any death camp in history.

'At first glance Auschwitz is like any other museum. Within the building, it's neat and tidy and well laid out. Visitors watch a short film. Not very pleasant, but the grainy black and white footage distances itself from the modern world. On a bright, sunny day the camp doesn't look too grim. Then again, no human flesh is being burnt, and thousands aren't being gassed by Zyklon B. My job was to remove any doubt about the horrors. I would make sure I read my script in my most monotone voice, keeping all my emotions locked deep inside me, same as I did with Hannah. There was no need to overdramatise the horror of my disclosures. I talked and walked, showing visitors individual glass cabinets full of battered suitcases, shoes and human hair. The shoes were particularly galling. Thousands of tiny shoes for tiny children's feet who took their tiny steps towards the showers. Most of the children were gassed on arrival. They couldn't work, they were too small and too weak. They had no value to the Nazis. There was no need for their existence so they stopped them existing. Over a million people were systematically slaughtered in gas chambers. Not just Jews from across Europe. But gypsies. The mentally ill. Communists. Resistance fighters. Polish people. Good Polish people suffered at the hands of the Nazis.'

'That's awful.'

'The Russian dictator Stalin once said one death is a tragedy, a million is a statistic. I'd show visitors the execution yard between blocks 10 and 11. I'd tell them trials lasted sixty seconds before the prisoner was stripped naked, taken upstairs and shot in the head. They'd have prisoners stand side by side and shoot them in the head with one bullet to save ammunition. In Block 11 we lined up in single file to walk through damp silent stone corridors to cells where four men would be forced to stand the whole night in a confined space measuring four feet by four feet. They would have to carry on working the next day. This would go on for days, weeks, until they were worked to death. The reasons for their punishment were equally insane, stealing food, slacking at work, being late for roll call. Prisoners hanging with their hands tied behind their backs, dislocating shoulder joints. It was torture for the sake of torture. There were no other benefits. It wasn't efficient or effective to kill this way. There were starvation cells where prisoners were held without food or water. I would tell them about the Franciscan Maksymilian Kolbe, who volunteered to take the place of another hostage and survived two weeks before they administered a lethal injection. There were dark cells with solid doors and tiny windows where prisoners would gradually suffocate as they used up all their oxygen. Sometimes a candle would be lit in the cell to speed up the process. At the end of the tour,

I'd show visitors the hanging block where the Nazis hung prisoners, usually during roll call to intimidate the others. I am sorry, I should stop this horror story. This is not appropriate for someone as young as you.'

'Go on,' says Summer. 'I've read about these the Nazis. I know many very weird kids in America idolise them. I've watched *Schindler's List* and cried. Jesus would want me to be a witness, same as you. That's why I am committed to the International Redemption Agency, finding love through forgiveness.'

Cain nods and squeezes her hand. Her eyes are red raw and tearful and probably match his. Is chatting to her helping him contextualise his desire for retribution? Or is he just playing nice, being kind and useful to a kid who thinks she can prove her faith by wearing a tight tee shirt with Redemption in big letters across her chest?

'Revenge against the Germans was swift, but not extensive. The first commandant, Rudolf Hoss, was executed on the same gallows outside the crematorium. About forty, maybe more, were executed. Two dozen more were sentenced to death by Polish authorities. Most of the six thousand SS guards walked away free as birds, assimilated back into society without punishment or censure. We have a habit of letting guilty men walk free.'

'You should be proud of what you did. It's a big tick for my future stepdad to be a caring man, making sure people cannot deny the holocaust. Why did you stop doing the tours?'

'Stress. I started doing it for the right reasons until it felt like I was punishing myself, like you just said, and I stopped. You had to be there to understand,' says Cain, knowing Summer is on the verge of joining the Serious Grief Club if April doesn't pull through.

'Because of Hannah?'

'What happened at Auschwitz is far worse than a road accident. If the hit and run driver had stopped, maybe my grief would have been less. Industrial killing in the millions ... just over 70 years ago. Survivors of the camps are still alive, yet people celebrate Hitler like he's a hero.'

'Do you know who did it?'

'I did. Then I didn't. We don't want to revisit it.'

'OK, shall we get back to my mum?'

Cain smiles, glad to get back on less traumatic territory where his emotions aren't being stretched to breaking point time after bloody time recreating horrific memories. This bit is fun and carefree, recalling the good times when everything was a hedonistic haze.

'April wanted to run a restaurant to put her recipes to the test, I could do the marketing, and she wanted to go back to Manchester where I was born and bred and she had visited and stayed in the nineties, meeting and marrying Bob. Although she was an American girl born in the USA, raised on promises, she hated what her country had become and feared where it was going as it lurched drunkenly to the far right under Trump and his enablers. I was in love and didn't care where I slung my hat because somehow April, your mum, had diluted my grief. It was amazing, I felt like a new man starting out with a fresh slate wiped clean.'

'And the restaurant, why call it the Red Manifesto? I am asking because I want to work in marketing one day,' says Summer.

'It is our project name. Manifesto because this is the blueprint for the perfect restaurant in our eyes. The one where we would want to eat and drink if we were given the choice. Red because it turns out we both loved Manchester United and we both supported the Labour party. And we both liked red wine. We must have tried out a thousand names before we reverted to the first. Broken Stones was the only serious contender alongside Life's a Beach. The brand name has hints of communism too, nods to Russia and China and Marxism. Crossing communism and capitalism was a very clever post-modern ironic marketing trick, if I say so myself.'

'What did she say about me, if she ever did?'

'Only that she had a daughter called Summer Sands Ord who lives with her film producer father in Hollywood because there were more life opportunities for you in America than with your shambolic hedonistic mum,' says Cain.

'She never asked me if that is what I wanted,' states Summer. 'Were you ever interested in meeting me? Two years is a long time to date somebody and never meet their only child.'

'You'd have to ask your mum about what you wanted, I am not good with kids and parents.'

'Why?'

'I lost my only child and my parents early doors and I am officially an orphan.'

'Do you want to talk about them? I've just proved I am a good listener with your tales of Auschwitz, horrible as it is.'

'I've never discussed Hannah with anyone apart from when it happened and for a few weeks afterwards. Never mentioned her when I exiled myself from Manchester. When people ask if I have kids, I'd lie. Say I fired blanks. Easier than explaining...I'd lost her while I was on the phone.'

'Did you and mum talk about her when you fell in love?'

'No. I left in Manchester in the Spring of 1998 to escape my little red dress, not to spend every day being reminded of her. My conscience couldn't take it. We knew about our respective bereavements but kept them under wraps,' says Cain, knowing he is repeating previous conversations.

'I am very sorry. Really sorry,' says Summer.

'Don't be. It's not your problem,' replies Cain.

'I feel it is.'

'Let's have some quiet time. I've talked too much. Why not say a silent prayer for all three of us?'

'Silent?'

'Silence is golden, you're too young to remember the song.'

'You know the International Redemption Agency can help you through your grief, spiritually and through counselling,' says Summer.

'Like Alcoholics Anonymous? Nick says God's 12 steps puts him off rehab.'

'It's not about an actual 'God', not for me. I am an intelligent woman, and I know 'God' does not have to be a religious entity, just a higher power, such as nature, or simply what happens when people come together to help each other. The International Redemption Agency is my replacement family. Dad failed me. Mum failed me. Everyone fails me. Do you want to ask me six questions about my life? See the real me? I can see you really care, and I want to share my thoughts with you.'

'We've done enough heavy duty lifting for one day. My head's ready to explode,' says Cain.

'What does your revenge for Hannah's death look like?' asks Summer.

'I don't know.'

'Do you want an 'eye for eye, and a 'tooth for tooth'?'

'I don't know. I dream of violence. I dream of poetic justice. I dream of seeing their pain,' says Cain, unsure what will satisfy him. It all depends on his mood, whether he is up or down or shuffling sideways in no direction.

'The bible says do not resist an evil person. If anyone slaps you on the right cheek, turn to them the other cheek also,' says Summer.

Cain grips her hand tight and glances over at April, thinks Summer is having the right conversation with the wrong person. Hopefully, one day...she can sort out her parental issues with her mum. Before he can frame an answer about not taking the bible literally, Vince finally calls, and Cain excuses himself from their bedside vigil.

Outside Cain sits in the same chair in the corridor where he had spoken to Rita Mann earlier in the week. Vince apologises profusely for missing Cain's call. Cain says he knows what Lucy Button is like when she is on a pleasure mission, he has personal experience before Vince, after all. He asks Vince to thank Lucy for her apology about what happened last night in the Red Manifesto when the two women were slap happy.

Vince says he would when she wakes up and asks what happened by the canal and Cain explains yet again. Vince double-checks the Swastika tattoo detail and says he would ask around his mates and fellow members of the Manchester Door Control Union. His instincts say Lucas Bone, a racist thug with McGinty connections. Maybe Billy is looking to add the Red Manifesto to their protection property portfolio and the attack is a new business drive. Vince asks Cain to give him 24 hours to find our more and then he'd have another chat this time tomorrow at the restaurant after it has reopened.

'We're closed until further notice,' Cain says.

'That's a bad business move. Stay shut for 24 hours like you've done, then open again. Cody can manage with my help. We need the money to pay our bills and mortgages, and our customers will want to support April once the story hits the front-page news. You know how the media works. And the mentality of the people it feeds. Bet you've already spoken to Matt Stark.'

'I can handle the media, that's aways been part of the day job. How do we deal with the McGinty family?'

'Like I said, give me 24 hours. We can catch up tomorrow.

I think you need protection from Billy McGinty in case they try again. I can send a couple of the team around to cover your back,' says Vince.

'Nick Forti is staying with me until further notice,' Cain says, lying instinctively, not wanting to be seen around Manchester with a couple of bodyguards dressed in black, sporting wayfarer Ray Bans and looking like gangster movie extras. 'Besides, it might only be for a couple of days.'

Cain explains about Bob Ord's California healthcare offer and new career opportunities in the film industry.

'Old Bob doesn't hang around catching flies,' says Vince. 'If you're going to Trumpland, I'd like to buy the Red Manifesto lock, stock and barrel before you go, mates' rates.'

'Never one to miss an opportunity Vince,' Cain replies, but doesn't tell Vince he only has a ten per cent share of the business, everything else belongs to April, the building, the fixtures and fittings, the cash that kept the business afloat during its initial launch. Everyone thinks the Red Manifesto is under equal co-ownership, but April holds the purse strings and has the final say, not that they ever argue about the Manifesto's direction. They never argue about anything, two fools pretending to be in love.

'Anything else?' asks Vince.

'No, we're sorted mate. Tomorrow.'

Cain could ask Vince why in his opinion a dying man took the rap for something somebody else did. Been ultra bold and ask straight up if he knows if Bob Ord killed his daughter. Cain could ask the same question to Ted Blake's widow, Len Harvey, and, probably Lucy Button. Cain still might, but if he did, they would simply clam up, tune into radio avoid and ignore him. A cover-up has lasted twenty years and the guilty aren't going to disclose their dirty secrets just because Cain asks them nicely. He has to be more subtle, tease the truth out of them one by one, then name and shame, see where that takes everyone. Will justice be improvised on the hoof, Saddam Hussain's chaotic death, heckled and hung by the neck until bones snapped or Colonel Muammar Gaddafi sodomised with a bayonet before he was shot or Romania's Nicolae and Elena Ceaușescu executed by firing squad before they could be lynched in the street? All three executions available online for posterity, no proof of their guilt needed. His situation is different, he needs to know beyond any reasonable doubt.

Cain has the perfect plan in mind. They host another party at the Red Manifesto to celebrate Bob's return to Manchester and April's recovery when they announce that she is heading for California. Cain could invite Bob's friends who helped make *All Down the Line*. That is a good excuse to knock on anyone's door. Everyone loves a good party, especially if there is a free bar and scran and a chance to look good and show off. He'd metaphorically punch them in the mouth and see what happened to all their smart-arse plans. And expose Hannah's killer once he has definitive proof. He'd better get the invites out and reverse his order to keep the place shut.

Twelve

That night the three of them are too exhausted to do anything other than slum it in a million-pound apartment. April's bed status is critical but stable. At home, Nick prepares a couple of dishes for the next two days, emptying the fridge and most of the freezer, but not the wine rack or the drinks cabinet. He is almost stone cold sober with an embarrassed grin on his face when they return. He explains he's cooked bland cottage pie with a Guinness and coffee chilli option. There is enough green veg to feed a rugby team with apple crumble and custard for afters. He's finished off a couple of bottles of Tom's cider and the half a bottle of the Irish black stuff not used in the food, says he is grateful for the temporary roof over his head.

The four of them eat at the table and decamp to the TV room, briefly discussing to stream either *All Down the Line* or the post-Brexit war epic movie *Dunkirk*, where plucky Brits turn a potential catastrophe into a great pyrrhic defeat. They have a quick vote and the latter wins unanimously. Bob says April is an extra in Line and they agree it is too upsetting to see her. Cain has never seen *All Down the Line* but makes a mental note to watch the movie as soon as he can to see what secrets it might reveal, if any.

That opportunity comes earlier than he thought when everyone has gone to bed, and he is alone in a double king-sized bed April and him bought when they moved into the apartment. He thought they'd rented it at the same time as signing a twenty-five-year lease for the Red Manifesto. A couple of months later he found out she'd paid cash, and she owned their penthouse castle in the sky, except she doesn't. She has secret sleeping partners other than Cain.

In the early of the hours, he finally watches the movie that changed Bob and April's lives. *All Down the Line* is funny, seeing Madchester's infamous sons impersonating the Rolling Stones and replacing the chug chug of early seventies rock with their own soaring, chiming guitars, funky bass lines and driving rhythms and confrontational out of tune vocals. Songs that soundtracked a previous generation capture Madchester's euphoria, youthfulness, energy and optimism. Cain finds himself tapping his feet and drumming with his fingers in the bed, listening to the music through expensive BOSE headphones.

The story is about laying down the track *All Down the Line* when somebody steals the band's drugs and follows the adventures of two road crew as they attempt to replenish supplies in Nice, bumping into all sorts of dodgy characters looking to rip them off. Several times Cain spots familiar younger faces amongst the extras in bar, restaurant, beach and hospital scenes, April and Violet, both heavily pregnant, non-speaking waitresses and nurses in a hospital accident and emergency department, Ted Blake drinking at the bar, Bob driving a taxi, Len Harvey working the door control at a seedy underground nightclub with Billy McGinty and Vince Crane backing him up, art imitating real life.

Once the film ends, Cain watches the inevitable DVD extras. In one clip, they are interviewing Bob outside the chateau in the car park. In the background, three people — Ted, April and Violet — are getting out of the black golf with a French numberplate. They are carrying shopping bags. Cain is too tired and exhausted to process anything beyond making a mental note to watch it again when he isn't so zonked.

Thirteen

Next morning Cain is up early doors, showers and shaves, and tiptoes out of the apartment with Summer and Bob still sleeping. He leaves a note for them, scribbles in barely legible handwriting that he has a few urgent errands to run that cannot be postponed. He will see them later in the morning at the hospital. They are to call him immediately if they hear any news, good or bad.

As Cain is about to leave, Nick whispers to him from under his duvet on the sofa. Asks if Cain needs him to do anything, help out in any way beyond the kitchen. He appreciates sleeping under a roof and not getting soaked or his nuts frozen off. Does Cain want him to speak to the police? Give them a statement about what he's seen. He could go back to his stomping grounds around the gyms and boxing clubs in North Manchester and do some snooping, try and find the names of the three muggers. He would happily hurt them to avenge April. All he needs is the nod and he would do it for free.

Cain is half listening and tells him if he stays more sober today than the day before, he'll be chuffed.

'Tell Summer we'll catch up soon. We had a pretty heavy conversation yesterday afternoon and I don't want her to feel ignored. Tell her we'll speak soon as I can, and I'll listen to her answers to my six questions.'

Nick gives Cain a thumb's up from under the duvet and says he will, as long as she doesn't try to press gang him into joining the International Redemption Agency. He doesn't want to end up playing trombone in a street band wearing a bloody military uniform and calling everyone 'Sir' like a gimp.

'That's the Salvation Army with military street bands. Not the IRA. Humour her, she's feeling lonely, and her mum is in a state.'

'And what about you, how do you feel Cain?' asks Nick. 'Are you OK?'

'Fine,' says Cain, an automatic reaction every male adopts when they want to avoid revealing how they really feel. 'It is what it is.'

'I could try and find the engagement ring. There are always dodgy black-market deals at the boxing gyms and pubs I used to inhabit in Moston and Radcliffe. I could ask around and see if I can buy it back if you give me some cash?'

Is it worth a punt? Cain says check the restaurant's social media feeds, there are bound to be pics posted online after his proposal. The two grand cash is still untouched in the kitchen.

'That would be great,' says Cain, thinking two grand is a suitable fee for rescuing the ring. 'See you around. 'There are a spare set of keys near the front door, if you need them.'

Half an hour later Cain has breakfast in Stevenson Street and catches the tram from Victoria to Prestwich via the Altrincham to Bury route. He hasn't been in this part of Prestwich for twenty odd years, but he finds the street and the house were Ted used to live without any trouble. It is a quarter of a mile from where Hannah was killed, and cold sweat drips slowly down his sides.

He knocks on the green door and a mature red-faced lady in a bright green leotard answers; her face is sweaty, a pink headband keeps her soaking hair in place. In the background Cain hears a confident voice telling the listener that dancing to the sounds of the eighties new romantics is the best means of keeping mentally and physically fit.

Cain last saw her twenty years ago when she let him and Harvey into her house so the duo could talk to her dying husband in a tiny box room. Somewhere along the line, time and money have transformed the timid mouse into a confident cougar who, like Arthur Seaton, looks up for a good time wherever she can find one.

Cain thinks he's changed from the callow youth armed with a tab, a pint and a cutting wit that sailed close to the wind. Sensible clothes rather than colourful. Less hair on his face and his head. A number one cut hiding the creeping baldness that first appeared in his late thirties. It is very doubtful she recognises him as the same man.

'The answer's no, no matter what you're selling,' she says, a semi-flirtatious smile reveals expensive bright white porcelain teeth that glisten as the morning sun.

'Sorry for disturbing you. I am not selling anything. My name is Cain Bell. Does Ted Blake still live here? I am an old friend of Ted's from his music and film days. He used to live in this house. A mutual friend, Bob Ord, is in town for a short while and we're having a surprise reunion party for him at my restaurant in Castlefield. Thought it would be great if Ted could join us at the Red Manifesto. Is he in or do you have a new address for him?'

'He died twenty years ago. His ashes are in an urn in the house. Never found time to scatter them.'

'I am very sorry to hear that. Are you ...his daughter?'

'Dorothy Blake. His widowed wife. All my friends call me Dot. Come in. Any pal of Bob Ord is a pal of mine. Do you want a coffee?'

'Sure.'

The house has been transformed as dramatically as her appearance. The end terrace has undergone a massive makeover since Cain was last here, threadbare carpets, second hand furniture and mountains of nappies and wipes for adults and for babies all gone.

She turns the Keep Fit video off and makes coffee in the kitchen. Cain looks at the framed pictures; Ted gurning with Madchester icons like Mark E Smith, John Cooper Clarke and Mr Manchester himself, Tony Wilson; Ted on films sets; Ted boozing and partying; Ted with the actors and production crew on *All Down the Line*, forty odd people in front of a decaying chateaux in need of a lick of paint. Cain recognises the pregnancy gals, April and Violet. Bob. Ted. Vince. Billy. The guys from the Roses and the Mondays. The drummer from Durutti Column. And Len Harvey, wearing a high vis yellow jacket that said 'security' on it. Odd that Len Harvey never told him he was on the film set.

Cain snaps the framed Line group picture on his mobile and notices the large wooden casket containing Ted's ashes. Cain's half of Hannah's ashes are scattered across Europe. He doesn't know what Mandy did with her share. They don't talk anymore.

'Nice shrine for your late husband,' Cain shouts to her in the kitchen as she boils the kettle and sings Maria Mckee's *Show Me Heaven*.

'He crammed a lot into a short life. More than most,' she shouts back, sounding proud.

'Including taking the blame for something he didn't do,' Cain says, undern his breath, out of her earshot.

'Shivers down my spine,' swoons Dot. Cain saw the former Lone Justice singer perform at Manchester University a couple of weeks before Hannah died and she refused to sing her biggest hit, too commercial. He applauds the courage of her convictions, but would have liked to hear her sing it anyway

Alongside the framed pictures, various souvenirs behind glass doors include backstage passes and lanyards, plectrums and set lists, tour programmes and school exercise books.

'Do you mind if I have a look inside the cabinet?'

'Be my guest.' She comes back with a French press, a warm jug of milk and digestives. 'I miss him so much. I never remarried. He is irreplaceable.'

'How did he die?' Cain asks.

'Cancer. Pancreatic. Quick. Less than four months from confirmation of the diagnosis.'

'Must have been tough?'

'It was. He was a self-employed sparks. When he got ill the money dried up damn quick. Friends stepped in from unexpected places. Helped us pay the medical bills and living expenses. Helped me with his funeral costs.'

'That's kind of them.'

'I thought he was hopeless with money, until I found he'd been saving up big time for a rainy day.'

'People surprise you.'

'I thought he was a right slack sod, but it turned out he was a planner. He even had life insurance. Never told me about that. We get a monthly sum. Never have to work. I volunteer for food banks. And do a shift or two a week for the Samaritans.'

Cain looks at other images around the shrine. One is a framed pic of a young timid Dorothy and a gaunt Ted holding a young baby shortly after his birth. There is another where the baby is several months older and cancerous Ted looks like an Auschwitz survivor. That must have been around the one-time Cain saw him, days before he died.

'I bet your boy is a man now.'

'Girl. Twenty, Jessica never knew her dad. Too young for any memories. Ted was in south-east France at the time filming in Les Salles-sur-Verdon in the Provence-Alpes-Côte d'Azur region and missed the birth. Sounds such a romantic place, an old creaking chateau hosted by impoverished French aristocrats. We were going to go there on holiday.'

'When was Jessica born?'

'Second of September, a couple of days after Princess Di passed. Ted flew back three days later, and I collected him from the airport to hear his bad news.'

'News?' Cain asks, picking up an exercise book and flicking through the handwritten scribble. Not only was Blake a sound financial planner, in his spare time he was also an anonymous Samuel Pepys who kept journals about his life on the road.

'Soon as he landed, he apologised and told me straight off he was dying and there was nothing to be done.'

So April's right. Ted Blake couldn't have been in two places at once. One question Cain never considered springs to mind: how come Len Harvey never checked if the alleged driver was in the country when Hannah was killed? Two answers: he always knew it wasn't Ted behind the wheel, or he was a lazy incompetent detective. Either option could be true, and both are morally unacceptable for a police officer and a so-called friend.

'These books are fascinating.'

'Ted kept tour and film set diaries. Said they would be his

pension. Said nostalgia paid because people wanted to relive the best years of their lives.'

'Is there one for 1997?'

'I am sure there is. He kept them for four or five years. Ian Hunter's *Diary of a Rock'n'Roll Star* inspired him. Do you remember him, the curly haired old bloke who sang *All the Young Dudes* without a hint of embarrassment at being so ancient looking himself?'

'No, not really.'

Cain picks up the seven exercise books, shuffles them like a pack of oversized cards and finds 1997.

'Can I borrow this? I have a few contacts in the book trade. If I share Ted's words with them, you never know what might happen.'

'Take them all. They have sentimental value, but there is no rush. When's the party? Is it impolite to ask for an invite for me and a friend?'

'No, of course not. You don't ask, you don't get. Give me your number and I'll call or text you soon as we confirm a date at our restaurant. I'll give Bob your regards. And Billy McGinty,' Cain says.

'The Grim Twins, as Ted called them. Grim and Grimmer. I've not seen Billy since the funeral. Almost twenty years ago. I bump into Violet down the gym. We always nod at each other. Jessica and Ryan went to the same school, were in a band together for a while, I think it is called the Angel and the Ass. Jess works for one of Violet's mates in a tanning studio in the city.'

'Have you read them? These diaries?' Cain asks.

'No.'

'Why not?'

'Never liked reading. Or writing. Shit schooling and parents who would rather smoke weed than bring up their kids.'

'Do you know what's in them?'

'Boys being boys, I would imagine. Chasing skirt and highs in-between grafting. Ted told me about his tours, turned me on with all his stories, but I never let him know. Too immature to make a show of myself with more than one person at a time. I am different now. That's why I stay in shape. Men don't want to bounce a sack of spuds. Women don't like flabby bits. What about you?'

'Just got engaged.'

'Congratulations.'

Five minutes after saying goodbye to Dot and her neat Kingwood Road terrace, Cain is upstairs in Costa Coffee in Prestwich village, the half-way point between her house and the tram station. A younger Cain might have responded to Dot's crass pass, but reading the diaries is his priority, not puffing the dust. Somewhere Ted might reveal his daughter's killer and the bastards who helped cover up his cowardly crime.

.

Fourteen

Skimming through the pages it is clear Ted Blake considered himself to be at the heart of the Madchester rave scene, a roadie almost as influential as the bands themselves, feeding vicariously off their morning glory. He had worked for the Mondays, the Roses and Oasis and complete unknowns who didn't have the songs, image, luck or smart management. When Blake wasn't gigging, he dabbled in film work thanks to his friendship with Bob Ord. Cain flicks through the journal until he reaches entries for the filming of *All Down the Line* when the Manchester music scene decamped en masse to the French Riviera for six long hot summer weeks. According to Ted, several of the city's drug dealers nearly went bankrupt and were forced to sign on during filming.

Ted was a funny man, but would his exercise books confirm the fiction of his confession? If Cain is lucky, he is about to find out.

Have another bust up with young Vince because he aint pulling his weight even though hes meant to be working for me!!!. Not even sure hes a qualified electrician like he told me when I introduced him to everyone. He keeps getting electric shocks. The bugger will get the same IMDb film credit as me yet I am doing his graft. Not fair so I tell Bob who tells me to man up. We all have to pull together. Says his own pregnant wife is busy cooking scran for the crew when she (April) should be putting her feet up. I tell him April is top scran merchant. Could do it for a living. Says she will be busy enough feeding four mouths at home once the twins arrive. He says Vinces 'pick me ups' is keeping the crew working long hours... just as important to him as sparking. Tells me we got to work night and day to finish the bloody movie or he is bankrupt. He can barely sleep at night...Fortunately Vince helps him sleep too same as he helps me and my bloody aching back which is getting too painful to endure. Been getting worse for two years now. Dot says I should see the doctor but what would they do????? Give me a bloody aspirin????? Stick a finger up my bum????? Still should not complain. Working on a film set is far better than humping shit on and off stage every night at the speed of the sound of busyness.

Life on a film set, thinks Cain. Vince is doing a bit of dealing way back when like he does at the Red Manifesto, small scale, mates of mates. April is busy cooking and working and being pregnant with the energy of a marathon runner. And the writing is on the wall for Blake with his aching back, although he did not know it. Bad back Ted's comma and apostrophe free prose, slightly reminiscent of Cormac McCarthy's *No*

County for Old Men, is about to get scarier with the arrival of 'Mad Dog'.

Bloody hell. Billy McGinty turns up with his heavily pregnant wife Violet who is due same time as April at the end of September. Bob wants me to collect them from Nice airport. Thats an hour I got to sit with the two of them in a bloody jeep. I am trapped with a fucking lunatic who breaks legs for fun. Story goes he made an associate swallow a Samurai sword in a Nippon restaurant in George Street and fed Jimmy Bone to his dogs on a squash court. Crazy bastard. Ive developed a stutter. I am so nervous. I keep on farting. Thank christ we are in an open top jeep. Len Harvey, our film set security guard, comes with us. Hes huge and calls everyone son like Johnny Cash even though hes dead young. Tells great stories about being a dibble, some of them horrifying.

Clearly Billy McGinty terrified Ted. Cain almost feels sorry for him having to chauffeur a violent psychopath around the south of France. Cutting up mates with a sword and feeding them to the dogs isn't reasonable behaviour for anyone. Read on...

Chauffeured Billy to Nice to pick up a car, a black Golf thats the dogs bollix. Hes making me so dead nervous that Ive suddenly got the flu and constipation to add to my intolerable aching back. Hes relaxed without his wife on his case and we chat like two blokes down the pub. I tell him I am due tests results from a French hospital but Bob is on at me to keep on working and get the results in England after the shoot finishes. Billy says hed speak to Bob about the check up. No point taking risks with your health.

Ted is not well and Billy's showing a compassionate side

to him. Maybe Violet is right, and her husband is just misunderstood. And maybe pigs will fly very high in the sky. Is that the same black Golf Cain saw on the Line extras last night? Is it the car that hit Hannah on Bury New Road? Probably, if they could ever find it.

Back ached too much to drive. My feet have got pins and needles and feel huge unlike my shrinking nob which wont stand upright for nowt anymore. April has to drive us to the hospital in a jeep. Len volunteered to drive us but he has to stop the cast getting too pissed and high. Shat myself most of the way. I have to remind her to drive on the right side of the road. April is a great cook but didnt concentrate or look at the road much. April is dead worried about Violet, who looks like shit warmed up. She says her kid has stopped kicking her. I am praying their waters would not break on the way whatever that means. Dot will tell me when we get home. Shes in the up the duff too. Huge sigh of relief when we reach the hospital. The two of them scoot off to the maternity unit double quick time. I went to see the cancer consultant who is going to tell me the pain in the back is a trapped nerve or poor posture. But I am not that lucky. No Sir. Not me. I have stage 4 pancreatic cancer and months to live. Turns out I am not the only one with medical challenges. Bob and Billy arrived. There are pregnancy problems.

Again, Cain almost feels sorry for Ted Blake. He isn't a medical expert but even he knows stage 4 sounds dead serious. And there is yet another lie to add to April's growing collection of massive whoppers. April says she did not drive because she is blind in one eye.

Twenty four hours later Bob and Billy explain to me that April has had an emergency cesarean birth and has a healthy young girl. Sadly a baby boy didnt make it. They called him Eric after Cantona. Violet has had a boy. Named him Ryan after Giggsy. The dead baby is our permanent secret and I mustnt say a word TO ANYONE INCLUDING DOT or I will be in the doghouse. Dont worry Billy I get it BIG TIME!!!!

Last entry.

More death. Vince tells me the Queen of Hearts is killed in Paris in a drunken car crash. Were packing up to go home but its taking to long. I want to see my new kid Dots called Jessica. I says I hoped Bob Billy April Violet and kids werent involved in the Paris crash and he says they were already back home. I says I hope we get paid in full because methinks Bobs probably over budget. Vince says why did he think Billy is here? For the suntan? He says Bobs a fool if hes borrowed from Billy M. Hes going to be paying top dollar interest. Not that Vince cares. As long as he gets paid, he doesnt care what he has to do. I am going to be dead skint if I dont work. My only legacy is a sad collection of diaries. Who is going to want to buy them!!!!!! Len says nostalgia will pay one day.

Straight from the horse's mouth, written proof Ted Blake wasn't in England when Cain's daughter died. There was nothing in it for him to make this shit up in a badly written book nobody is ever going to read or buy. Cain so wants to believe April is mistaken but Ted is off the hook and Bob is well and truly on it. He must have been the driver, him or Billy, one of the two?

Cain sips his coffee and a woman two tables down drinks her tea, engrossed in her mobile. He looks around the Costa Coffee in Prestwich, north Manchester, seeking a lanky child dressed in a little red dress. He buries his head in his hands and feels a dark shadow descend over him, blocking out the sun and the heat of a bright Mancunian September morning.

Fifteen

Big Vince Crane is standing in Cain's light, a look of concern on his face that evolves into relief. He gives Cain a big double thumbs up and glances momentarily at the road crew diaries.

'Am I pleased to see you,' he says. 'Where's Nick?'

'Day off.'

'Really?'

'We're a socially responsible employer.'

'...who gives his head of security a sheer heart attack,' says Vince, sitting himself down without ordering anything. 'It's bad enough dating Lucy Button without you adding to the craziness.'

Cain smiles to himself. On quiet days, when the Red Manifesto runs itself, the two of them would play backgammon and philosophise about sex, drugs, rock and roll, football, films and politics.

'They attacked April, not me,' Cain says, realising he was

deliberately shoved into the canal so he could not see what was happening to April.

'How come you're not with April?'

'Been visiting Ted Blake's widow. She lent me his unpublished *Diaries of a Rock and Roll Roadie.* You're in them?'

'Ted Blake gets precedence over April?'

'I always thought Ted Blake killed my daughter in a hit and run accident in 1997, same weekend Diana died. Turns out I was wrong. Somebody else killed her.'

Vince looks at Cain sharply, appears to be genuinely surprised by his revelation, and shakes his head slowly.

'Who told you?

'Ted confessed in person to me before he died.'

'You kept that to yourself?'

'I was sworn to secrecy.'

'He's dead, you don't have to keep your oath anymore. How do you know he is lying?'

'An anonymous caller marked my card a couple of days ago. The diaries prove both of you were still in France working on *All Down the Line* until the first week of September.'

'You accusing...?' asks Vince. 'That's a big-time mind fuck. That's very heavy. Who told you?'

'Like I said, an anonymous call. I don't recognise her voice before you ask,' Cain says.

'Before or after the mugging?'

'I cannot remember.'

'Jesus Christ, Cain. Shouldn't you be focusing on April, not chasing ghosts? You've been too busy watching fictional detectives.'

'It's OK, her family are with her. Bob the film producer and her daughter Summer. Although April's in an induced coma, she's stable,' Cain knows his excuses sound pathetic. If his love is unconditional, he would be there, holding her ice-cold hands and willing her to pull through, regardless of any elephants in the room. She's let him down and he doesn't really know what to do about it, yet.

'The usual?'

Cain nods and Vince stands up and gives the barista their order before sitting down again. They sit in silence and Vince flicks through the diaries like they are picture books. Cain wonders if Vince is smart enough to speed read or is he pretending to be interested while they wait for drinks and nibbles. A few moments later the barista hands Vince two coffees on a tray and chocolate croissants in a bag and thanks him for his custom and wishes them both a nice day.

'Seriously mate, you've got to forget about Hannah's death, it is two decades ago,' says Vince, the espressos look like egg cups in his huge hands. 'Let it go.'

'That's rich from a man who adores Ireland, wants to unite it, but lives in Manchester,' Cain says, and grins to show no offence is meant, the king of the spontaneous one liner is on top form. 'And still hates Thatcher with a passion.'

'You would too if she starved your mates.'

'You were too young.'

'Fuck you, Cain, that's not the point.'

They walk a short distance from Costa to Vince's black Range Rover. Cain rides shotgun while Vince steers the black beast out of the car park, turns left onto Fairfax Road and left again onto Bury New Road towards Manchester's city centre. Seconds later, they pass the spot where Hannah was hit and Cain flinches at the memory and closes his eyes tight.

'OK?'

'Tired and a bit stressed,' Cain replies, truthfully. 'I am only messing about Ireland.'

'I know. Banter bollocks between best buddies.'

While Vince drives, a text comes through from Summer asking when Cain is coming to the hospital. Soon, he replies. She texts again, Bob is busy with the hospital administrators and his insurance people. Cain replies, good and she sends a third text, says she is abandoned, despite their talk yesterday afternoon, and she has a proposition.

Vince asks what is going on and Cain tells him Summer wants reassurance and is playing text tennis with him like young women do. Vince laughs at the macho put down and says women are different to men, always like to talk and talk and talk. Nothing is ever off limits, not like the males of the species with manly rules, honour codes and walls of silence in sport, politics, violence and sex. A good mate looks away from poor behaviour, doesn't pass judgement, according to Vince.

Half a mile later Vince turns right into Heywood Road and heads towards Simister and Middleton. They stop outside a primary school on their left and a high school on their right. Vince kills the engine and looks towards eleven o'clock and 'Hacienda' villa that appears totally out of place in a north Manchester suburb. The house, dominated by a first-floor balcony that stretches along the whole of its width, was located in the landscaped grounds behind a brick wall protected by heavy duty barbed wire and glass and CCTV.

'On the outside, looks like the set from *Schindler's List*,' Cain says, picturing Spielberg's epic holocaust movie where the commandant of the Płaszów concentration camp, played by Ralph Fiennes, stood on the circular balcony of his home and randomly shot and killed prisoners he thought were slacking, work shy or not walking fast enough.

'Or the Maze in Ireland,' Vince, half grimaces, quick as a flash. 'But us political prisoners didn't have a large pond, small swimming pool, a tennis court and short par 3 golf hole complete with two bunkers, a manicured green and an elevated tee or JCB excavators on hand 24/7.'

'You were too young to be a Maze resident.'

'I was there in spirit the day I was born,' says Vince,

with a wink. 'I don't think your mugging is a random attack. Somebody is sending us an unsubtle message.'

'What do you mean?'

'Word on the street is Billy McGinty wants my security gig and your restaurant.'

'Why?'

'He can make a lot of money from the Red Manifesto. He likes to follow easy money, does our Billy.'

'Running a restaurant properly is bloody hard work.'

'Not Billy's way. Great place for him to deal drugs. Smuggle immigrants through the kitchens. Perfect business for cleaning dirty cash.'

'How do you know this?'

'Rumours about Billy's Manifesto ambitions have been circulating for several weeks now.'

'How come you never told us?'

'And the scare the shit out of the two of you? There're always stories circulating about McGinty wanting to stick his tongue in someone else's pie. Most of them are bollocks, to be honest. But attacking you and April changes the nature of his game.'

Vince never looks at me while he speaks, the usual excitement missing from his worried Irish lyrical lilt.

'Does he want to buy us out?'

'Under Billy's rules your name stays on the paperwork while he eats all the pies.'

'You're making this shit up.'

Vince shakes his head, cracks his knuckles loudly, like an old banger backfiring.

'I wish I was.'

'How do you deal with a madman like Billy McGinty?'

'Kill him.'

'Me?'

'Not you personally. You couldn't punch your way out of

a crisp packet. Hire somebody.'

Cain laughs at the absurdity of an idea that belongs in creative writing schools where published crime authors teach middle-class retirees to write about charismatic serial killers.

'I love your sense of humour, Vince,' Cain says, 'How do I hire an assassin in Manchester. Google? Facebook? TikTok?'

'I'll do it.'

'You're not a killer,' Cain says.

'I wasn't until I was,' grins Vince. 'Plenty of disappeared traitors would testify if they could speak. You'll have to read my memoirs when I write them. All will be revealed although I might have to disguise a lot of the players. Don't want to be a bullet magnet myself, you know what I mean Cain? The Irish have long memories, dating back to the great famine and way beyond. There are a lot of experienced killers out there. Once they've killed once, it's much easier the second and third times.'

'You've got a vivid imagination, Vince. Why would I want to assassinate Billy McGinty when I am leaving on a jet plane soon as April's fit to travel?'

'Because Billy is the driver who killed your daughter.'

Cain swallows hard and feels the lump in his throat choke him. He coughs a few times to clear it.

'How do you know?'

'Lucy told me. April told her. She knew all the time. Think about my offer. I'll drop you at the hospital so you can be by April's side, where you belong. Me and Lucy will be in touch with the proof about Billy. I am sorry Cain, you deserve better, much better,' says Vince, starting the Range Rover's engine.

Vince is right. Cain deserves much better, from everyone, including direct answers from Billy McGinty. He grabs for the passenger door handle and pulls it open before Vince can activate the central locking mechanism. Cain squeezes his tall frame out of the passenger seat and palms off Vince as he tries to restrain him. A passing car beeps furiously as it narrowly avoids the open passenger door. Cain ignores the driver and starts out across the road towards the McGinty farm, unsure how he is going to climb over a two-metre brick wall's lacerating glass and barbed wire. He can forget hoisting himself over the walls, the gates at the entrance are the obvious choice. Just before Cain reaches the gates, he is rugby tackled from behind and feels himself tumble to the ground like a sack of spuds. Dogs bark furiously on the other side of the wall.

'Don't be silly,' whispers Vince into Cain's ear. 'This is what he wants. A reaction. You're easy pickings. Do it my way. A bullet to the back of his head. None of that careless messy Massey slaughtering with spitting Uzis in public places. You break into his compound his dogs will rip you to pieces.'

Vince is lying on top of Cain, his sheer weight pinning him to the ground. They are the same height, but Vince is a third heavier than Cain and works out religiously in the gym five times a week. The Irishman flips Cain with ease and holds him in a bear hug. Vince gently squeezes and demands Cain surrender before his ribs break and lungs pop.

Cain backs down.

Vince picks Cain up like a cat carrying a young kitten by the scruff of its neck. When they are both on their feet, he dusts himself down and Cain does the same.

'Don't ever do that again shit for brains,' says Vince. 'How can I protect you in this crazy world?'

Cain thinks trying not to snap his ribs and burst his lungs is a good starter but is too knackered to say the words as he tries to control his breathing and reduce his heart rate.

Cain looks up and sees a couple on the balcony look in his direction, non-plussed by two grown men wrestling in the streets. They wave a couple of times and go back into their villa hugging each other in a show of domestic unity. Do they know it is Cain and Vince or are they used to seeing men jump out of cars and fight each other in front of their house?

Cain touches his forehead with two fingers and feels sticky blood from a graze and wipes them clean on a hanky. He looks at the McGinty household and the balcony is empty apart from a lanky girl in a little red dress waving at him. Cain closes his eyes and looks again, and she has gone leaving only tears running down his cheeks.

Sixteen

After Vince drops Cain at the hospital, he is tempted to catch a taxi back to Manchester, find Lucy Button and interrogate her about April's confession sessions, confirm if what Vince says about Billy McGinty is true. But much as he wants to find out the truth, Cain must be patient. He stands in the hospital entrance surrounded by seriously ill people carrying metal drips stands intravenously feeding them drugs while they smoke cigarettes as if tomorrow no longer belongs to them.

Anyone looking at Cain averts their eyes when they see him muttering to himself. They don't want to be involved with a nutter. They have enough problems of their own to deal with without taking on another heavy load.

Cain tells himself to stop acting the spoilt brat with a face like a smacked toddler's bottom. He should grow a pair and go check in on his fiancée, find out how she is doing.

Summer is sat with April in ICU and invites him to join her. Still shell-shocked from Vince's revelation, Cain numbly pulls up a chair and listens and nods frequently while she explains her old man is on a mission talking to hospital admin staff. It is going to cost a small fortune and promises to be a logistical and medical nightmare, but if anyone can make happen, Bob is your man. She says she's never been prouder of her father, going against his self-obsessed nature to leap into action to support his estranged wife. In their hour of need, Bob has finally come to the party.

'Is it time for my six questions about your life and times?' asks Cain as he watches Summer nipping at the fleshy part of April's hand. Cain's eyes flick from her hands to her face and back again, thinking she is obviously her mother's daughter, but her face reminds him of someone else. 'Why are you pinching her?'

'Extra insurance. I — we — want a reaction. I've spoken to a couple of the nurses. They told me that happens next,' says Summer, her voice full of the optimism she normally reserves for her prayers to her God.

'And what's that?'

'They are going to start weaning her off her medication now the swelling is less severe and see if she wakes up naturally.'

'That's good news?' Cain asks, thinking for a second April is going to come around in her own good time. Everything will be resolved...if she has a memory left.

'Yes and no,' Summer pauses, doubt in her voice. 'The old man's pissed off and paranoid about the doctors wanting to turn the machines off before we have permission to move her to America.'

'Understandable,' says Cain, hoping Summer does not think freezing her dead mother is sane behaviour.

'If she's brain dead they might say no.'

'How do they decide?'

'Apparently two senior consultants will carry out a series of medical tests independently or each other. The results have to be 'negative' of any sign of brain activity before they can clinically and definitively say life has ceased. Once the effects of the drugs have worn off, they carry out tests. See how she responds to a light shone into her eyes. They are looking for reflexes to the light. They'll touch April's eyelids and eyes with a gauze to see if her cornea reacts. They'll apply cold ice water to her ears for any reaction in her eyes. They'll use pain stimulus, different areas of the body, try and provoke any facial reaction. The slightest, smallest reaction will prove her brain is still functioning. Although she might be in a comatose or in a permanent vegetative state, she is not dead. If she doesn't respond to any stimulus, their final and definitive test is to disconnect her from the ventilator when an absence of breathing is confirmed by a blood test to measure the carbon dioxide and oxygen levels in her blood. If April's carbon dioxide levels in the blood increase, the brain stem is dead.'

'So that's why you are pinching her hand?' asks Cain.

'I am waiting for the miracle God is sending our way,' whispers Summer. 'I can trust you one hundred percent, Cain. We both want the same thing, don't we?'

'Sure,' Cain says.

'Are you going to help me, Cain Bell?' she asks, her voice barely audible, rasping with emotion.

'How?'

'We tell them she responds to our touch.'

'Who?'

'The nurses and the doctors.'

'Has she?'

'Not yet.'

'I thought God demanded only the truth from his flock. The International Redemption Agency too?'

'Yes, but he is OK with white lies if they are for the greater good. This will be our secret. But we never, ever tell anyone. Not even Bob. Not even mum when she recovers and is back living on happy hill.'

'How are we going to fool experienced doctors?'

'We tell them separately when we are alone with her. Two totally unrelated instances. They cannot call us both liars. Once she is on that plane, they can whistle Dixie until the cows come home.'

Cain looks at April sleeping, blissfully unaware of her own plight, laughing at him. Would she be proud of her ex-husband and her daughter cheating, lying and deceiving? The sad answer is yes, April embraces a natural disingenuousness that runs in the family.

'I am not adverse to a few little white lies. It's the giant big hairy ones that hack me off,' Cain says, ready to be her accomplice in deceiving the nursing staff and doctors.

'Do you know any really bad ones?' asks Summer.

'One or two but they are not for sharing yet,' Cain says. 'When is this going to happen?'

'Whenever the drugs are out of her system. They're not saying exactly when. They don't want to get sued for making wrong statements. Sorry. I am sounding like Bob.'

'That's OK. Nobody should be going through this trauma at your age,' Cain says, and he realises that anyone seeing her and Ryan together would come to the same conclusion. It is so obvious. Cain thought Ryan looked familiar when Rita Mann showed him the snapshot and now he knows why.

'What's up?'

'Nothing.'

Cain ignores her and looks at her comatose mum, hiding yet another big bad lie from him. Was it done on the snide, a clandestine affair, or were they swingers, shagging each other? One thing is certain, Summer and Ryan are brother and sister in the eyes of any reasonable person. Do they know they are siblings? Although DNA provides definitive proof, Cain needs to confide in someone who has no sense of morality, a guttersnipe like him without a conscience. Only one person springs to mind: Lucy 'Doll Face' Button. Time for him to pay her a visit and make good her promise to talk about why her and April were slap happy.

Cain tells Summer they will start weaving their little white lies as soon as April is free from drugs as their narrative should make medical sense. He'll see her back at the flat as he had work to do before leaving Manchester one more time.

Seventeen

A taxi ride takes Cain back into Manchester's small gridlocked city centre. He can walk up Deansgate faster, but wants to reflect on his history with celebrity psychiatrist Lucy Button before they reconnect privately. When Hannah died Cain was working on the daily news as a reporter alongside Matt Stark and his future wife Grace Marsh. The newspaper's editor, Michael Shields, said the publishing group would pay for six counselling sessions with Lucy to help Cain cope with his trauma. Lucy had her clinic and her apartment in St John's Road, a posh quarter of the town midway between the Castlefield basin and the newspaper's head office in Deansgate. Their generosity didn't extend to Cain's wife Mandy, who found help in the arms of a lay preacher called Brett, an auctioneer in Australia, ten thousand miles and a million light years from here. Brett always boasted

Scientologists, Mormons, Christadelphians, the Salvation Army and the International Redemption Agency were too middle of the road for his liking.

At first Lucy is good. She appears to be on the ball from the moment Cain and her kick off the first session. He asks how he was meant to cope with Hannah's death, and she spoke with an honesty that he found refreshing after weeks of being smothered by bleeding hearts saying they knew how Cain felt and constantly asked if he was OK. She told him that although his recovery officially started with this one-hundred-and-fifty-pounds per hour conversation, there were no quick fixes to mend a broken heart. Bereaved people tried to return to normality far too soon. They forgot to give themselves the proper space and time to grieve and mourn. She says he would be traumatised for weeks, if not months or years, before the actual grief set in so he doesn't need to worry his sorry arse about trying to articulate his feelings or apologise to her or anyone else, including his wife, his boss and his friends and colleagues. If Cain wanted to be moody and morose, he had every right to be pissed off. She held Cain's hand and said she wanted to reassure him he'd come out of this, no matter how bad he felt right now. She would be by his side for the entire journey for as long as he needed her. She told him he needed to wait at least a year, or possibly longer before he accessed effective therapy that would help him grieve properly rather than the current superficial sticking plaster sessions they were pissing about with at the newspaper's expense.

Cain asked her how she knew that would work.

She said time healed her when her husband drowned on holiday in St Lucia. She was on a private beach, waving at him while he swam and waved back, or so she thought. He was crying out for help as the water sucked him under. She never blamed the hotel or the travel agent for not warning them about the treacherous water. They should have known, except they were too much in lust to find out. Now, seven years on, she doesn't remember his ordinary everydayness. Nor his smell. Couldn't really remember the sound of his voice and she refused to watch their wedding video or look at old photographs. Fortunately, he died before social media became an obsession. She did occasionally dream about him screwing her, an inappropriate memory trick for Cain to use as Hannah was his daughter. But Lucy liked imagining her husband's big hard cock inside her. She said she was a Freudian thinker – not in the boys shagging their mums' sense — but she did believe dreams reflected true wishes. Part of her wanted him back, although she knew that would never happen. Was she being too blunt?

That interaction took fifty-nine minutes. She said they had a minute left of their session before she finished for the day, and did he fancy a drink upstairs in her apartment, listen to some original Skynyrd or Free with Kossoff and have a toke or two?

They completed the six sessions without discussing Hannah too much by simply avoiding the couch after sixty seconds and going straight upstairs for 59 minutes. They smoked, listened to the blues and held each other and she let him cry in her arms in between strokes, caresses, little kisses and sips of Jack Daniels. She was the only woman who saw him cry over Hannah. They didn't get it on sexually until the third week and by the sixth she told Cain about her second love and could he sub her for a hundred quid until a cheque cleared. Her dealer didn't give her credit anymore. That was twenty years ago, and she is still going strong, isn't bankrupt or tricking as escort or on the streets, or homeless like Nick Forti, an original street survivor in every sense of the word.

Cain and Lucy saw each other for six months once or twice a week. His marriage disintegrated faster than the space shuttle Columbia when retuned to earth with a few missing tiles and disintegrated on TV. Lucy comforted him as best she could, but would not stop her habit, despite numerous requests. Disillusioned with women, work and a wasted life, Cain left Manchester for new beginnings away from the tragic city, armed with a ruck sack, credit cards and a *Rough Guide to Europe.*

And here he is, outside the front door of her clinic, wondering if the keypad entrance number or is still the same? He rings the intercom for the office several times, there is no answer. She is closed for business on a Tuesday. Not good for business.

Not that it matters, she probably crashed out in a drug-induced stupor.

Cain enters the four-digit pin and door opens with ease. It is amazing she has never been robbed given her guttersnipe lifestyle. Maybe Vince protects her in ways others cannot, his name and reputation are enough to keep angry dealers at bay.

There is an alarm, but that isn't switched on. She never had CCTV installed because she wanted to protect client confidentially. She is a crazy mix of wild child and responsible adult, randomly flitting from age 16 to 66 without warning.

The downstairs clinic rooms are all locked. The computers on the reception desk are switched off. The wooden filing cabinets locked too. Everything else is neat and tidy. Nothing out of the place. A showroom for shrinks.

The keypad four-number code to access her apartment upstairs hasn't changed either. Cain keys it in and walks up a staircase lined with certificates of medical achievements and press cuttings. It is a well-kept affluent pad for a single girl in her late forties with an expensive heroin habit.

Cain glances around the kitchen and the lounge for anything out of the ordinary. Her mobile is on the wooden coffee table in the middle of the room. Cain picks it up and inspects the screen. He tries the four-digit code that opened the doors but it doesn't unlock the Lucy Button's digital secrets and dodgy contacts. Apparently Apple only allows a certain number of attempts at a password before it locks the mobile for good. Without a password, accessing her digital world remains secret for an eternity, unless the tech boys are lying about the security of their apps and systems.

He puts the phone back on the coffee table, enters her bedroom and sees her naked on her back, unconscious on the bed, a needle in her left arm, a black leather tourniquet tied tight above it. On her bedside table, her works are neatly laid out, a methodical addict who co-existed with drugs for decades, until now. Light shines through the open curtains and onto her Doll Face, giving her an angelic glow, unblemished white skin pure as porcelain contrasts with reddish blood mottled death patterns. Rigour mortis has stiffened her body. Everything is slightly unnatural, unposed.

'Fucking hell, Lucy. What have to done to yourself?'

Before Cain can phone an ambulance, he hears voices from downstairs laughing and joking, like Oasis about to rehearse after an afternoon session down the pub. Lucy didn't associate with rat boys when he knew her intimately; her dealers were white middle class yuppies like her. Cain is immediately wary as one of the voices sounds like Swastika Boy from the towpath. He isn't going to hang around to say hello and find out if his assessment is accurate. He hides himself in a fitted double-doored wardrobe. Hopefully his thumping heart is not giving his secret hiding place away amongst the luxury dresses, coats and blouses and silk chemises. Cain takes out his mobile to record their incriminating words, he wants a contemporaneous record to corroborate what he's seeing and hearing. He turns on the video player.

The smell of weed precedes them. He sees them enter the room through the slated doors, cupping long spliffs in their hands. They are not surprised at seeing a dead woman in her morning glory, a spike in her arm, like a character from a Lou Reed ditty in his sleazy seventies prime, Lucy Says.... she's gonna to watch the blue birds fly...

From his vantage point behind the cupboard door's wooden slats, Cain's initial assessment is right about Lucy's surprise visitors. The tall one is Ryan McGinty. His mate is Lucas Bone has tumbling dice tattooed over the Nazi ink, his face and eyes look like he's gone ten rounds with prime-time Nick Forti.

'She looks very dead, our kid,' says Swastika Boy.

'Jesus, Lucas. She sure smells like death.'

'Dead fit, like that stubborn April Skies bint hanging onto her life,' says Lucas. 'We should call her the Coma Chick after that Joe Strummer bloke my old man used to play. I'd give her one too lying there unconscious in a bed surrounded by loads of horny nurses watching us fuck.'

'Sands. Her name is Sands,' says Ryan. 'And she's not a bint.'

'Calm down lover boy. We're only having a laugh. Here, photograph me and take a bit of video!'

Lucas whips out his big dick, strokes it slow and hard like he is acting in a porn movie. He lewdly points his long cock inches away from various Lucy Button orifices and adopts extravagant sexual poses.

'You're dreadful Lucas Bone. You'll be visiting the morgue with the ghost of Jimmy Bone.'

'Don't diss the old man. Not his fault he likes sniffing dirty knickers and and hosting chemical submission parties.'

The two of them giggle like schoolboys, Mancunian versions of Beavis and Butthead modelled on Liam Gallagher and Mark E Smith.

'No head shots, we can sell these necrophilia specials online.'

'Do they pay more for dead people penetration?'

'You'll need lube.'

What is wrong with these people and whoever they share these horrific images? Cain wants to throw up but that could prove fatal.

'Spit roast time? Get your dick out Ryan and we'll both bone her.'

'I'll carry on filming. A money-shot would be good TV. But get a move on, we've got a train to catch, Berwick-upon-Tweed waits for no man.'

Cain thinks they cannot get any lower, but they do when Lucas ejaculates over Lucy Button's face and chest and rubs his sperm into her cold flesh like it was an expensive moisturiser. At least he hasn't stuck his dick in Lucy like that awful Lone Justice song written by Tom Petty, what was it called, *Ways to be Wicked*?

'Right let's set this place alight, then we can go collect our merch from Berwick upon Tweed, give us a couple of days for this Skies shit dies down.'

'April Sands. That's her name,' says Ryan.

'Who cares?'

'I do.'

'It was an accident,' says Swastika Boy.

'You sure?'

'You were there. How did we know her brain would bleed?'

They both throw their spliffs on the bed and wait for the duvet to ignite.They are there, but they aren't.

'Welcome to Lucy's funeral pyre party,' says Lucas.

'And all who burn with her,' says Ryan.

Does that include Cain? He is trapped in the room with two perverted psychopaths, hidden in the closet, trying hard

not to throw up, recording man's inhumanity to a Doll Face
for posterity. What he's just witnessed can never be unseen.

Eighteen

During Cain's lowest moments in the aftermath of Hannah's death, he often thought about taking another way out. In his head, he'd see himself scoffing fistfuls of pills, slashing his wrists, walking into the cold North Sea, jumping from a bridge over the M62, although truth be told he suffered from pretty bad acrophobia, ironic given his own height. Leaping in front of an intercity express was out of the question because it would traumatise the poor driver when his face splatted against his window. The only other exit he never considered was burning himself alive. That was too painful and horrific to imagine. What if some do-gooder extinguished the flames and he had to live with the agony of half of his flesh burnt off? And here he is, irony of ironies, hiding in a wardrobe, watching two dipstick pyromaniacs film themselves incinerating Lucy.

'Must look natural. Nothing suspicious,' says Lucas. 'But burn her. Burn her good like the Protestant bitch she is.'

Cain thinks Swastika Boy does a good job impersonating Gerry Adams or is it Ian Paisley or Martin McGuinness or even Vince Crane? The Irish all sound the same with their high shouty voices, irrespective of their God and politics.

Bizarrely, Cain's Generation Z arsonists are chilled teens who fancy themselves as alternative stand-up comedians doubling up as political impersonators. Are they that disassociated from society that there are no limits to their depravity? If it is in the genes, Summer is in trouble if Ryan is her twin.

Not that he has time to worry about his future stepdaughter's mental health. His life is about to get very hot, smoky and uncomfortable.

'We need to give this little bonfire a boost,' says Swastika Boy. 'Grab some of her shit from the cupboard that will burn dead fast.'

Shit, the bastard son of Billy McGinty is coming towards him and is going to expose Cain's hiding place. Cain has one advantage, Ryan isn't expecting him. What did Nick Forti tell Cain? Everyone has a plan until they are punched in the mouth! A great idea, if you punch them hard enough so they cannot retaliate. Cain grips his car keys in his right hand, a makeshift knuckleduster to jab into Ryan's face to bust him up good and proper.

Ryan's hands are on the handle. He is looking through the slats. Can he see Cain who can see Ryan? Have their eyes locked? He is Summer's spit, but he isn't pretty like Summer, he too appears to have gone too many rounds with prime-time Nick 'Thor' Forti.

Not that there is time to pontificate about twins. The door is about to open. He pictures hitting and running like the wind until he reaches the safety of the basin and Vince

Crane's security net.

But the door never opens.

Does Ryan recognise Cain? Has he even seen him? Just because Cain sees Ryan, how does he know for certain Ryan hasn't spotted him in the dark recesses of the closet? Ryan stares vacantly ahead into the void, emotionless.

'Don't worry,' says Swastika Boy. 'I've found her soiled dirty underwear.'

'I'll get some alcohol from the kitchen. That will help,' Ryan says. He walks away from the cupboard and out of the room. Through the slats Cain sees Lucas sniffing Lucy's knickers and the bras and suspenders from a laundry basket before tossing them onto the burning bed.

Less than a minute later, Ryan is back in the room, pouring a bottle of brandy over the dead shrink's smouldering corpse. The small fire on the bed responds to the accelerant with gusto, flames dance towards the ceiling. Ryan adds her phone, whatever secrets are held on the device are about to disappear for good, unless they are backed up in the invisible cloud.

'Job's done. Let's go.'

'I need a shit,' says Lucas. 'Curse this bloody constipation. I'll give myself a bloody hernia trying to squeeze the big one out.'

'Second door down. And put the wood in the hole. I don't want to hear you straining like a beached whale.'

Lucas grins inanely and leaves the room and Ryan goes over to the window. Unlocks it and slightly opens it to add oxygen to spread the flames. He makes a call and leaves a message, 'everything is tidy. We're leaving now to drive to Berwick. Staying at the Rob Roy B&B overnight as agreed. We'll collect the hardware and the gear. Back in 48.'

And he makes another short call and repeats a similar message with subtle differences, 'I feel dirty after what we've just done. We're off to Berwick for hardware, dodgy meat and some gear. Any news on me mum? Text me? Back in 48.'

Lucas is back into the room and locks the door behind him, leaving the key inside the bedroom to fit their accidental fire narrative. They go to the window and climb out, leaving Cain locked inside an inferno.

Cain waits and counts and waits some more until he has no choice but to break out. The cackle and hissing of the fire are louder, his escape route determined before he opens the wardrobe door. He plans to follow them out of the window and hopes they aren't waiting for him to beat him to a pulp.

He opens the cupboard door, Lucy's body is burning and smelling like badly burnt pork The ceiling and curtains are burning fast, and the flames are spreading, Cain's vision and breathing are going to be seriously impaired by the thickening smoke within seconds. Can he extinguish the fire, give her family enough charred remains to incinerate or bury, at a later date.

No chance.

He must go now.

Cain moves fast, keeps low, black tee shirt pulled up over his mouth and nose, like they do on the telly. He tries not to inhale while he races to the window and lifts it up, swinging a leg out. He balances himself on the sill and looks at where he can land. There is a twelve-foot drop onto either concrete or an expensive dented black BMW parked in the backyard with Beavis and Butthead footprints indented on the roof. Cain jumps feet first onto the car and hopes he isn't going end up a paraplegic or worse. Shockwaves jolt through his body. Cain tries to roll with the jump and keep his balance, like an Olympic gymnast dismounting from the parallel bars. His score is an imperfect seven. Both knees hurt, but he is still standing. He climbs off the mangled car roof slowly and is grateful when his feet touch solid ground.

Cain catches his breath and glances around him. The two arsonists are gone. Cain takes his mobile from his pocket, dials 999 and asks for the fire brigade. Tells them he can see flames coming from an apartment in St John's Street. Other people in the area will be calling 999 too, the emergency services would be here soon. Does he stand up and be counted or stay anonymous?

Cain has until the police arrive to concoct a credible story that could not be contradicted by the filmed evidence of nosy parkers from behind twitching net curtains. If he looks ridiculous enough jumping from the burning building, his escape could go viral within seconds, and he would look a right tit lying through his teeth. To be honest, looking stupid on the social media is the least of his worries. Wanking and ejaculating over a cadaver and filming themselves is truly sick.

To make matters worse, Cain is convinced Ryan has seen him, but is unsure why the son of 'Mad Dog' says nothing? Had Ryan expected Cain to die in the flames, locked in Lucy's bedroom? Is Ryan that callous and clever to eliminate the witness in a bonfire? Who is the mum he'd talked about? April or Violet or somebody else? Why would Ryan let him go? In a perfect world, Cain would discuss this dilemma with somebody he could trust with his life. Twenty years previously, he thought he was surrounded by friends who had his back. Now there is nobody in his corner. Just him, himself and his absolutely barking confused mind.

Perhaps he should throw caution to the wind and call Rita Mann and let the police deal with criminal activities beyond his comprehension. The evidence is taped and stored on his mobile and automatically synced with his cloud account. Can he convince Rita to give him a glimpse at the Hannah Bell folder in return for the tape inside Lucy's flat? Although he is no lawyer, he guesses burning and sexually assaulting a

dead body, possessing weapons and hardware are all strictly
no go.

Cain needs a drink to soothe his red raw throat and give
him time to think, clear his head to make the right decisions.
He quickly walks away from the fire looking for the sanctuary
of a bar and a beer and a packet of pork scratchings.

Nineteen

Cain scoots down back streets of Manchester to the White Lion in Liverpool Road opposite the city's science and air & space museums. He orders a pint of Timothy Taylors and scratchings. He finds a corner to hideaway from a couple of sullen solo regulars, one reading a newspaper and the other doing a crossword. Two groups of chirpy tourist foursomes sit and laugh around tables in the window bays, rubber necking as sirens wail and red engines and blue lights flash down Liverpool Road. One of the lone drinkers finishes his pint and wobbles out of the pub to follow the chaotic noise of the emergency services. He leaves his daily newspaper on his table alongside his empty pint pot.

Cain goes across the pub and picks up the tabloid, free in the city centre because the internet and social media mean newspapers are virtually worthless. He sits down again and sips his pint and savours its citrus peel aromas, malt and grassy hops with marmalade sweetness and a long bitter finish. How do southerners drink pints without a decent frothy head? He slowly chews on pig gristle and silently toasts the death of a woman who helped him, however badly, through the biggest crisis of his life. Lucy Button had numerous faults, but she was essentially a good egg gone too soon, although some might say she did well to last so long with her bad girl ways. Have her secrets gone up in smoke or are they stashed away somewhere? Who would know?

Matt Stark's press story about April's attack on Sunday night is in print. Good to his word, he follows their agreed narrative. He quotes an anonymous spokesman from the Red Manifesto about April's family being by her bedside. He plays down the seriousness of her injuries in line with the police and medical authorities. April is 'critical but stable', until the celebrity chef isn't.

Cain knows his underwater mobile would be pinging like crazy from the bottom of the Rochdale canal as friends and colleagues read the news and reach out to commiserate and wish him all the best. There are plenty of messages on April's too, but he ignores them, including multiple messages from the London agents, Shelley and Fiona, but they can wait, like everyone else.

Apart from one.

Nancy Hood has texted several times and asks Cain to call. He rings back and she says she is after a quote about a story she is going to syndicate about April and him. Unsurprisingly, Nancy is in a far more amicable mood than when Cain last spoke to her, no longer click-bait curious after Matt's word in her ear about the McGinty connection.

'Hi Cain. I am writing a good news piece about the friends of the unluckiest man in Manchester coming to his rescue in his hour of need.'

'What?'

'Lightning striking you twice in the same city. Losing

your daughter twenty years ago in a car crash. April being seriously hurt in a mugging. Your friends have set up a Go Fund Me page to help pay for your trip to the USA to the Emily Frances Head Injury Clinic in Los Angeles. Raised two thousand pounds already. People are very generous when the chips are down. Film financier Bob Ord's paying for April's medical care and another Manchester exile and fellow film producer, Howard Rich, has appointed you as his studio's head of social responsibility. Good to have such positive news to offset the negative. Do you have a comment about the kindness shown by everyone?'

'This isn't your usual modus operandi, Nancy? You're more gratuitous salacious shit. What's going on?'

'I've had a religious conversion, my wooden buddha is shedding tears in my loo. I joke Cain. You know I've always loved human interest stories. By the way thanks for your off-the-record warning, I have heard a lot of bad things about our mutual friend. I've been gang banged once against my will, Cain. Don't want it to happen again to me, or, worse, to my daughters. I am never going to mention the subject again, ever. But I owe you one. Now, what do you want me to say about your friends helping you go to the US of A?'

'A big thank you to the NHS and emergency services who have come up trumps again. The staff at the Red Manifesto have been magnificent, as has April's former husband. Bob Ord, and their daughter, Summer. Hopefully we'll get April back in the kitchen as soon as we can. She's a strong determined woman. I'll be taking her up the aisle as soon as she is fit again.'

They both laugh in embarrassment at the implied crudity of his otherwise bland on-the-record quote, the sort of thing people say at award shows when they thank everyone they know, including the nannies dragging their kids up when they were absent being famous and difficult. Like Summer, thinks Cain, missing good times with both her mum and her dad because they were too busy to care. Not like him with Hannah, always on tap to support his daughter, whether it was sports, school productions or singing.

'Thanks again Cain and good luck in America,' says Nancy. 'And keep off social media. All sorts of daft rumours abound about you and your motivations, none involving my handicraft. You know how toxic it is. You got a cold? Your voice sounds very hoarse?'

'Probably man flu,' quips Cain.

The line is cut and Cain calls Matt straight away to thank him for the coverage and for helping Nancy.

'The police are playing the attack right down at their press briefing. No detail at all about any suspects and the 'critical but stable' is reported verbatim without any further explanation. The police are quoting an anonymous hospital spokesperson. My editor Sally Bailey says I can only report the severity of her injuries if somebody — you or the hospital or the police — go on the record. Is she still in danger?'

'Yes,' Cain says. 'We'll find out more over the next 48-hours.'

'The police reported another mugging near the Rochdale canal on the night you and April were attacked. Two unnamed youths beaten up by a tall white man and a short black man. Nobody's going to pick up on it, but you know the score. Somebody is getting their retaliation in first.'

Cain does know the score and thanks Matt for the info and explains about the move to the USA and the clinic to treat April.

'A permanent move?' he asks.

'What would you do if you were me?'

'I'd be searching for my passport ... but I'd want to sign the contract first.'

Safety conscious Matt, thinks Cain, disingenuous Matt,

scared Matt. Always getting anything to do with money in writing. Matt is big on having contracts. He is the best reporter, crime or otherwise, Cain has ever met and should have been a national player rather than sticking in the provinces, a big fish in a small bowl, Tom Courtenay in Keith Waterhouse's *Billy Liar*, not brave enough to elope to London with Julie Christie, deliberately missing the train as it pulls out of the station.

'We're having a goodbye party before we go at the Manifesto. Could be soon. They are keen to move her quickly.'

'I'll miss you, again,' says Matt. 'I thought you'd be back for good second time around.'

'So did I,' says Cain.

'No best man gig for me?'

'Never say never. April may recover sooner than we all think.'

'I'll pray for you two,' says Matt.

'Join the queue bending God's ear about little old me and the missus,' says Cain, picturing Summer railroading Nick into accepting help from the International Redemption Agency. They are at home, chomping on a takeaway pizza and sharing a family-sized bottle of coke and ice cream for afters. Bob would be squirrelled away in sitting room, working his mobile as usual, setting up financing deals for USA productions, shouting out good morning to his fellow movie megalomaniacs across time zones even though Manchester is deep into another evening.

Cain orders another pint, unsure what to do. Are Swastika Boy and Ryan McGinty on their way to Berwick, four hours up the M62/M1/A1? There is a tiny window of opportunity to catch them red-handed with whatever merchandise they are smuggling across county lines.

One call satisfies his moral duty, although there is no

legal obligation to report witnessing a crime, as far as he is aware. Just educate Rita with one sixty second phone call.

One call.

Give her his necrophilia recording and tell her he was in the room witnessing the debauchery. He doesn't know who they were. He couldn't see their faces or recognise their voices, but the sound speaks volumes. In exchange, she gives him the name of the driver of the black Golf? One call sets the ball rolling towards the hole.

Yes, or no?

He dials.

Rita answers second ring.

'Hello Cain. How can I help you?'

'Are you working?'

'I could be. What's up?'

'Can we have a chat in person? I've got something for you, if you've got something for me,' says Cain, ready to barter sexual perversion for an archived open file.

'What?'

'Dynamite.'

'In English? Stop teasing me.'

'Evidence that will turn your stomach.'

'That's not intriguing enough. Tell me more.'

'Two people of recent interest to you are impersonating Jimmy Savile in return for Hannah's file or the name of her killer?'

'Can you stop talking in riddles? What's this got to do with Jimmy Savile?'

'I'll swap a perverted 'morgue' sex tape in return for Hannah's file?'

'Where are you?'

'At the Red Manifesto.'

'Give me half an hour.'

'With the file?'

'An approximation.'

Cain doesn't know what she means but agrees anyway and closes the call. The mobile rings again, the screen says Len Harvey, finally reacting to Cain's voicemail. Probably on the lash with his creaking drinking buddies, geriatric dinosaurs on the pop pretending they are still relevant and not yesterday's men.

'You OK, son? Long time no see. I got your message and listened to your allegation.'

'Hi Len. Good to hear your voice too.'

'Sorry to hear about your fiancée, April. Did they arrest anyone?'

'I am not in the loop. Same as Hannah all those years ago.'

'How come you're a disgruntled man who wants to rewrite history.'

'I've got a few questions for you about Ted Blake.'

'Fire away, son.'

'Better face to face. You still living in Manchester? You know I run the Red Manifesto in Castlefield,' says Cain.

'I've heard, a bit too posh for me, out of my price range. Bit disappointed you never got in touch after all I did for you, son.'

'Bad memories. You know how it is.'

'Not really,' says Harvey. 'I thought what was said in the room, stayed in the room?'

'Let's talk face to face,' says Cain. 'I'll be...'

'I know how to find you, son,' interrupted Harvey. 'See you in a bit, but don't be a smart arse, son. Don't forget, I've stopped you once from making the biggest mistake of your life.'

'I was only joking.'

'Were you?'

The line is cut. Harvey sounds like a Mancunian Johnny

Cash minus the sense of humour, not that Cain needs his funny bone rubbing. He just wants the truth about the driver. He'd never been close to stabbing Ted Blake, although he might have suggested the idea to Harvey more than once. And he did carry a special Japanese Miyabi 24cm Gyutoh Knife in the boot of his car for a few weeks, ostensibly to learn how to cook food like the Teppenyaki restaurant in George Street in city centre Manchester. He only threatened Blake because he thought that was what grieving fathers did, according to blood-lust revenge movies.

Cain calls Summer again and tells her he will be home in a few hours. He is still putting his affairs in order before his permanent goodbye to Rainy City, says he is looking at selling his share of the Red Manifesto to a friend. He says he'll update her tomorrow when they pinch an inch with April, and he asks her his six 'get to know you better' questions.

As they are about to end the call, Nick interrupts and asks if Cain is OK, they have seen the fire engines from up high in the Beetham Towers penthouse and know that Red Manifesto is in the vicinity. Cain says it is close to the Red Manifesto where he is working, but not to worry. He'll be back as soon as he can and not to delay eating because of him. Nick says food is the last thing on his mind and he needs to catch up with him urgently about buying jewellery from Diamond Dave. Nick says he'll meet Cain down the Manifesto if he is struggling for time. Before Cain says hold your horses, the line is dead. Nick sounds excited and a bit pissed. At least he's gone back to the apartment and not done a runner with Cain's two grand float.

Twenty

Cain closes the door of the White Lion on Liverpool Road and turns an immediate left into one of the few remaining green spaces in city centre Manchester. The centrepiece of the Castlefield Urban Heritage Park is a few bricks from an old Roman fort that has somehow become a clever 'tourist attraction' even though there is hardly anything to view or experience beyond a very active imagination. Cain wants to enjoy the fresh air and decides to take the long route to the Red Manifesto rather than skirt under the Castlefield viaduct. He turns another left into Bridgewater Street and right into Deansgate and right onto the Rochdale Canal towpath.

Alone, he crosses under Deansgate 100 and stops and looks up at Beetham House, his apartment almost knocking on heaven's doors. He was happy there with April, living the life in the sky, and now it is all over, suddenly ripped away from him without warning.

Cain saunters along the towpath, the smell of burning in the late evening air. He glances over at the homeless camp on the other side of the water and imagines he is Marlow in Joseph Conrad's *Heart of Darkness*, fighting through deep, dark river jungles in search of Kurtz, a petty tyrant, a dying god, an embodiment of Europe's dark side and brutality. He closes his eyes and pictures the dense foliage facing him, the restless natives hidden from view ready to attack him, except Manchester's homeless are away from their makeshift homes, visiting soup kitchens, begging or robbing to stay afloat.

There is movement from the bushes, and he sees a rifle barrel stick out from the undergrowth, hears two muffled noises in quick succession, not loud or sharp enough to be live gunfire. Although no expert, the pfft pfft sounds like an air rifle. There are fresh indents on the wall three or four feet to his right around his shoulder height.

Is someone trying to kill or scare him? He hasn't been hit. Hasn't even been close. Cain twists his feet forty-five degrees, backs up against the wall, arms spread wide like Jesus on the cross.

'Come on, come on, come on,' he shouts to whoever is shooting at him from the other side of the canal, grinning at the insanity of it all. 'Come on, think I am scared of you and your little air rifle, Billy?'

He holds his defiant pose for a full and very slow sixty seconds until his outstretched arms ache and he drops them with a sardonic grin. How many silly warnings does he need when he's already decided he is taking the money and running, accepting an offer that is too good to refuse.

'You sick motherfuckers, go fuck yourselves. Is that the best you can do, Billy?'

Cain digs out the spent pellets embedded in the wall which have become flat round disks with traces of their skirts still visible. He puts them in his pocket. Must have been kids messing about with air rifles, a pure co-incidence. A cold-blooded killer like Billy McGinty doesn't piss about with an air rifle to threaten people, that is like tickling somebody into submission with a feather duster.

By the time he opens the Red Manifesto's big floor-to-ceiling glass doors, he decides it is kids being stupid. His attackers are on their way to Berwick and are not a threat.

He steps inside and turns off the alarm system and switches on the lights over the bar and the dining areas and ensures the closed sign is clearly displayed on the entrance. It is funny standing by himself in the middle of a restaurant that caters for 200 covers and employs forty odd full and part time staff.

He walks through the door marked PRIVATE - STAFF ONLY and enters a large open plan back-office space. He sits down at the security station and logs onto the CCTV system to switch it off for his private conversations with Rita. The system is already turned off and has been since the previous Saturday night, the day before the awards event and April's attack. Another co-incidence or has it simply broken down and nobody has had time to fix it? He'll have a word with Vince, check what has happened, except it doesn't matter, the Red Manifesto is no longer his business. Is there a manual for the CCTV system in one of the drawers? He opens a couple. They are full of badges and lanyards, radio phones and earpieces, typical security paraphernalia. The third draw has a neatly folded Boddingtons Bitter bar towel hiding the contents underneath. Cain lifts it. There are a couple of knuckle dusters, two iron bars wrapped in black tape and a gun that looks like an old World War 2 weapon, although Cain is no expert, not like some of his obsessed gun freak mates who get the horn playing with replica pistols and machine guns.

Cain closes the drawer instantly and pretends he hasn't seen the weapon. What is Vince doing leaving anything unlocked in an office, his office in a business he and April own? That is crazy. They'd be shut down instantly if anyone knew.

He draws his breath and opens the drawer again and inspects the weapon without touching it. Anecdotally, he has heard it is five years for possessing a gun. A neighbour in north Manchester got 12 years for selling a pistol and supplying chemical submission sex drugs.

What is it doing there?

Is there a legit reason?

Maybe Vince has confiscated it from a punter and forgot to hand it into the police. Cain shuts the drawer again and leaves the back office. It is a good thing the CCTV is switched off. He feels the urge to light up, even though smoking indoors in public places has been banned and is against the law.

He pulls a pint of bitter from the hand pump and sips the chilled Boddingtons bitter, once the cream of Manchester brewed with water from a well running underneath the Strangeways brewery next to the infamous prison that graced the front cover of a Smiths album.

He sips the beer, grimaces at the imperfect pint that has sat in the cask too long. When Rita arrives, she is wearing a red jumper and jeans and wet hair tied up in a bundle on the top off her head, her face is free of make-up.

'I've had to postpone a night out with a hot young man. I was just getting ready. Not many civilians get my undivided attention, but 'Jimmy Savile' did pique my curiosity.'

'Do you want a drink,' asks Cain. 'A smoke?'

'Shall we cut the crap, Cain?'

He refills his pint pot with another half and gives her a half too. She doesn't need to drink it, Cain thinks it is rude to drink by himself.

'Cheers.'

'Good health.'

He invites her to sit down next to his dentist's chair at the end of the bar, underneath the Mezzanine. She accepts and he plonks his butt down, unsure how he is going to play this.

'Any news on April's attackers given the seriousness of her injuries?' he asks.

'No, have you given us a full statement?'

'Not have time.'

'Nor have Lucas and Ryan. Stalemate.'

'Funny you should mention them, have you got Bluetooth on your mobile?' asks Cain.

'Sure.'

'Let's pair our devices,' he says, taking out April's mobile, using the password to open the screen and settings. Within seconds they have paired up and he opens his file manager app and selects the video nasty from Lucy Button's bedroom. Cain taps the share button and selects Rita's device.

'What are you sending me?'

'You'll find out when you accept the transfer.'

'Tell me in your own words what's going on?'

'I've shown you mine. Now you show me yours,' says Cain.

'That's not going to happen. Sorry,' replies Rita, taking a small sip of her beer leaving a thin line of froth on her lip. 'You ask what you want to know, and I'll check. Best I can do without corrupting myself. Spoke to your friend Harvey. He says he would call.'

'He has. Earlier this evening.'

'I forgot to ask, how's April? I believe you're fast tracking her to America soon as you can.'

'They are trying to bring her out of her induced coma

over the next 48 hours. We'll see what happens.'

'You're holding up very well.'

'I am a veteran at dealing with post-traumatic stress disorder, once bitten twice shy, as the cliche goes. Listen to the tape. It's about 12 minutes long. I made it in a cupboard in Lucy Button's bedroom so there are no images beyond her dresses and coats. She is well and truly dead and naked with a syringe in her arm. Two men came into the room, and I hid in the cupboard. I didn't see any faces. This happened a few hours ago, there was a fire at Button's residence in St John's Road in Manchester.'

Rita listens to the tape on speaker on her mobile without commenting, holding the device up to her ear when the recording becomes indistinct or muffled.

'That's sick. Can you identity them visually?'

'No. I never saw their faces, close up, only through the slats. One of them sounded like Lucas Bone, the dude on the towpath last Sunday. Wherever Lucas lays his hat, Ryan McGinty follows. That's the best I can do.'

'They taped themselves sexually abusing a dead body. Did you actually see that?'

'Through the slats. I heard the noises the animals made, saw it too, but nothing on tape. Do you want me to describe what I saw?'

'No, not yet. I am so sorry you've been tainted,' says Rita.

'Me too. They are sick people and need punishing.'

'Agreed, one more question, why did you delay telling us?'

'Too shocked. I needed a drink in the White Lion to calm my nerves.'

'I understand.'

'I am not in trouble?'

'No.'

'What happens next?' asks Cain.

'We'll evaluate this information, this video evidence. I'll pass it up the food chain.'

'And will you act on it now?'

'Not my decision.'

'Hardware, is that a euphemism for guns?'

'We're speculating. We can only respond to the evidence we have in front of us,' says Rita. 'If there is a threat to life, the stakes get ramped up.'

'Billy McGinty won't know about this?'

'By the time he does, you'll be in California, well out of his reach.'

'Am I safe?'

'You've not been threatened or intimidated by anyone since?' asks Rita.

Cain thinks about mentioning the two pellets fired at him on the towpath of the Rochdale Canal, give her the lead from his pocket. The three and a half pints have emboldened him, and he rationalises killers don't use airguns to assassinate their enemies.

'Can it be off the record? Anonymous? When we first spoke, you talked about protecting me from Mad Dog and his pack of hounds. Is that still your priority?'

'I'll make a note of our conversation, no names attached for the time being. I understand you're scared, but any evidence is stronger coming from a real person. Leave it with me and we can chat again tomorrow. I'd really like a signed statement for the record, looks better in court, but there is no rush. Whatever you do, this tape is very useful, I can't thank you enough for having the courage to share it with me.'

'You could tell me about Hannah,' asks Cain.

'Nothing untoward is in the file. Everything's recorded and noted about Ted Blake being the only name in the frame. No action taken because of lack of evidence and his stage 4 cancer. We didn't get as far as talking to the CPS.'

'How did the police get Ted Blake's name?'

'A confidential informant,' says Rita, swilling the beer in the bottom of her half pint pot.

'No name?'

'Wouldn't be confidential then, would it?'

'What do you have?'

'Only his alias...*Straw Dog*. Apparently, he or she gave Harvey the info, who in turn passed it on to the investigating team.'

'Would you have investigated differently?'

'I'd have tried harder to find the car, the black golf with false number plates. Apart from that, nothing.'

'What happened to it?'

'We don't know. Scrapped or broken up and sold for parts. There are literally dozens of back street garages in North Manchester. Ted Blake would have known all sorts of dodgy people.'

'Ted Blake isn't the driver,' says Cain.

'Does it matter?' asks Rita and for one second her mask slips to reveal her unspoken truth. She isn't interested in what happened twenty years ago, that is ancient history in her world. Makes no difference to her who drove the car. She is interested in live cases. Crimes that are happening today or would take place tomorrow. The past is a less interesting country like Belgium or Canada.

'No other suspects. No Billy McGinty? Or Bob Ord?'

'Not on our radar.'

'McGinty lives less than a mile from the incident. No CCTV tracking the car?'

'It disappeared in Prestwich somewhere.'

'No motorway CCTV tracking?'

'Only the M62. The number plates were false.'

'Did it belong to McGinty or Ord?'

'False plates.'

'They have a black Golf on the set of *All Down the Line*.'

'Black Golfs are very popular.'

'CCTV of the car?'

'1997 technology, not as clear as today. We can't identify the driver.'

'Is *Straw Dog* Billy McGinty?'

'A good detective has lots of snouts. The more secretive they are about their identities, the longer they live in my experience. Any more questions?'

'You've stiffed me, received more than you gave,' says Cain.

'You have a clear conscience, that's priceless,' says Rita,

'And a guilty man drives on *Thunder Road*, steering clear of the promised land?'

'Very lyrical, sounds like Bruce.'

He thanks her for nothing and shows her to the Red Manifesto door. No matter what happens next, he's caused a bit of grief for two sick perverts, Ryan McGinty and Lucas Bone. The police can decide what to do with the information. One day the tabloids or salacious social media gossips will have a field day when it comes out in a court or online that two Manchester gangsters sexually assaulted a sexy naked dead woman before cremating her. They were in Jimmy Savile territory, the former Top of the Pops TV presenter and establishment clown posed with dead bodies in lewd positions, performed oral sex and bizarrely stole glass eyes for jewellery — and escaped justice, while he was alive.

Twenty-one

Cain thinks about ditching the gun in the water outside the Manifesto, but it is a dangerous undertaking if he is spotted, and the canal is drained. Maybe he should call Vince, let him take the risk. The pistol is in an unlocked drawer at his security station at the Manifesto, so it really is Vince's problem. When they do speak, does Cain tell Vince about the sexual abuse of Lucy Button? Would Vince take the bible's 'eye for an eye' justice literally and kill the two rat boys? Vince claims he is a killer. If Cain says nothing, his silence is complicity and he is no better than the people who look the other way when others are hurt or exploited, like the passenger sat next to the driver who killed Hannah.

Hypocrisy was a heavy burden. Cain's original emotional stress, Mandy Vickers, was a closet evangelical Christian, hid her faith until they were wed. Afterwards, she endorsed the bible wholeheartedly, agreed homosexuality was an abomination not to be condoned under any circumstances, except when she was very pissed once and kissed and touched her best friend's erogenous zones. The bible told Mandy it is OK to stop Cain having any contact with her body while she was in her monthly period of menstrual uncleanliness and gave her permission not to dine with him if he was thinking of eating shellfish or touching the skin of a dead pig.

If suspect bible and evangelical Christians don't have the answers, how does he decide what is justice? Act on instinct, respond to spur of the moment provocations, ask questions after any bloody retribution? Cain's problem is there is no one around anymore to discuss his conundrum. His previous support group is either too old, too young, too homeless, too cynical or in a coma.

Cain pours himself an orange juice, stares through the Manifesto's long glass floor-to-ceiling doors and windows and sees an outsized big bear lumbering towards him from across the bridge, dressed in black strides, black shirt, black overcoat, black Dr Marten boots, black gloves, black scarf, and a black Fedora felt hat. He is carrying a white polystyrene tray of chips as he swaggers towards the Red Manifesto, the bridge reverberating underneath his bulk. Occasionally he dips in and spears a chip with a wooden fork.

Cain opens the door and lets him into the Red Manifesto and glances around to see if anybody is with him. He closes the doors and forgets to lock them.

'Alright son,' says Len, offering Cain a long fat juicy chip from the half empty tray swamped in a congealing curry sauce. 'You're looking well.'

Cain declines the invitation to grab a curried chip, he isn't drunk enough for 2am scran.

'You too, big man, would never think it is almost two decades.'

'Landed on your feet with your own boozer. Can I help myself? Always been an ambition to be locked in a bar! Just need somebody to bring on the dancing whores and we're in heaven.'

Len Harvey walks across the restaurant floor to the bar, picks up a straight glass pot and pours himself a pint of Goat's Milk, the Manifesto's award-winning September guest ale, a refreshing bitter notable for its blend of pale barley, crystal malt oats and aromatic hops. Cain handpicked it a few months ago and it is selling well.

'Nice,' says Harvey, raising a glass to Cain and downing the pint in a couple of quick gulps without the beer touching the sides. Harvey belches loudly and mutters spiders under his breath before pouring a second pint. 'Got your message. Why are you raking up old history? Who is the naughty little bird with the big beak?'

'April Sands. She owns this place with me. You're drinking her beer. She's in a coma. The night we got engaged she says Ted Blake wasn't behind the wheel of the black Golf. Twenty odd years ago you told me he was the driver. Ted Blake confirmed it himself. Is she lying to me, her future husband? Or have you been lying to me all these years?'

'Phew, hold your horses, son. This is a lot to digest out of the blue,' says Harvey.

'Is it true?'

'You trying to catch me out, son, trip me up by getting me pissed on free ale?'

'I just want the truth.'

'Whatever I said to you back in the day was said in good faith. A lot of water has flowed under the bridge. If I recall, an informant gave me Ted Blake's name. I spoke to Ted Blake. He said he would admit it off the record to you as he was dying anyway. If we arrested him, he'd deny everything.'

'How convenient. Did you check his story panned out?'

'Why? When April says she loves you, do you try and prove her wrong or accept her word that she loves you? Mrs Harvey says she loves me every morning before we ride, I never doubt her commitment to our mutual pleasure.'

'I can prove Ted wasn't in the country when the crash happened. His diaries place him in France over that weekend in 1997. He was working on *All Down the Line*. You were there too doing security and acting as an extra.'

'Well done. Clever you. Round of applause for the amateur detective of the year,' says Len and he claps his gloved hands very slowly. 'What I do in my spare time is nothing to do with you, no offence.'

'I am being serious, Len, I need to the truth.'

'What do you want from me?'

'Just the name of the driver and the man sat next to him?'

'Why do you ask for such a thing when you know Ted Blake was the driver? Do you think I am corrupt? Easily bought? I thought we were good friends. You ever accuse me outside of this room, I'll snap your spine into fragments and the use your vertebrae as toothpicks!'

Len smacks his pint down on the bar and splashes half the liquid over the woodwork. Cain flinches at the sudden dramatic reaction from the angry huge detective.

'Sorry.'

'Only joking, son. You look like you were about to crap yourself. Don't blame you for asking me, but like that TV dirty copper in Northern Filth, Owen Chard or was it Billy Whyte, you're talking to the wrong man.'

'Why?' asks Cain, unimpressed with Harvey's inopportune humour.

'Your daughter's dead. Nothing is going to bring her back. I told you about Ted Blake and gave you peace of mind for two decades. If I was you, I'd forget what April says and carry on believing we both got the right man. Put it in a box and lock the lid. Walk away. Nothing's ever going to bring her back.'

'That's not fair.'

'Life's not fair, son. If it was, we'd all be hung like horses with an infinite capacity to sup beer and maintain an erection like an iron girder. Actually, I can do that. Lucky me.'

'Who is your grass?'

'Wrong man, again.'

'Billy McGinty?'

'That talk gets you hurt, son.'

'I am not sacred, not anymore. I've been battered and bruised too much. Lost everything.'

'Cheer up Cain, you're spoiling the good vibrations. Looks like your pet IRA ape has escaped his cage.'

Cain looks towards the entrance and sees Vince Crane's enormous pyramid figure peering into the restaurant through the unlocked tinted glass doors. The Manifesto's head of security enters the building wearing drainpipe blue jeans, snakeskin cowboy boots and a tasselled brown suede jacket like Jon Voight in the iconic gay *Midnight Cowboy* movie, surely a wardrobe malfunction.

'Hello Vince.'

'Detective.'

'Can I pour you a pint on the house, or on Cain seeing as he's here and he's ultimately paying. Goat's Milk, Guinness or Boddingtons?'

'I'll have a pint of black gold.'

'What brings you here tonight?' asks Harvey. 'More of Cain's comedic japes?'

'Saw the lights on. Just doing my job. I am fully licensed security operative registered with the city council, unlike your best mate. I am checking no lowlifes with Nazi facial tattoos have broken in or attacked anyone.'

Cain looks at Vince and tries to decide if he knows about

his girlfriend's death. Vince is relaxed, despite his antipathy towards Harvey. How do these things work? How do you drop Lucy Button's demise into a casual conversation? Len Harvey has no such etiquette qualms and plunges in headfirst.

'You look shit, Vince. Those sad tired eyes of yours are red raw. Presumably you've heard about the fire in St John Road? They found a body they cannot identify it's so badly burned. Were you seeing a bride there, that junky head shrink? Come in and get your pint.'

That is savage from Harvey, but Vince's expression doesn't change one iota.

'Thanks detective, it'll take a couple of minutes for the black stuff to settle, but well worth the wait. I'll just go and change my jacket. Bit cold out there.'

Vince saunters casually towards the PRIVATE - STAFF ONLY back-office door, rolls his massive shoulders while he strolls across, and disappears from view.

'I saw the fire and called it in,' says Cain.

'Is that why Rita Mann was here?' asks Harvey.

'Yes.'

'Were you a witness?'

'Yes. I was outside the building and called 999,' says Cain.

'You weren't asking Rita about Ted Blake, were you? You know she's not involved in the case?'

Cain hesitates to reply, unsure if it is a red rag to an angry old bull. Is he going to drop her in the brown stuff by saying she has discussed an open case with a member of the public?

'She is a good friend of April's, belonged to her book club. She consoled me at the hospital while April was having brain surgery. She was there visiting her sister.'

'And not talking about Ted Blake?' asks Harvey.

'No, Ted Blake talk,' lied Cain.

'Ted Blake?' asks Vince as he comes back into the main

restaurant wearing a large much looser leather jacket. 'What's he got to do with the price of cheese? We all know it was Billy driving the car, don't we detective and you let him off the hook, leading Cain up the garden path like the mug you think he is. I am his friend so I am calling you out. Deny it?'

Cain winces at Vince's stark challenge to Len Harvey, the two heavyweights bogging each other out, oblivious to Cain's presence.

'Are you man enough to accuse Billy to his face, Vincent?'

'Fuck off Harvey, you bent bastard. You think he's still employed by the police, Cain? Old pisspot Len's been impersonating a police officer all his life, giving his criminal bum chums a free ride.'

To be fair to Vince, he does have a point. Cain thinks Harvey is still a detective, just assumes he is, although he might also have passed compulsory retirement age and is living it large on a generous police pension.

'You shouldn't talk to me like this, son.'

'You know me,' says Vince.

'You're out of order, son,' says Harvey.

'You know me, you know what I am like.'

'You'll regret this.'

'Not as much as you. You know what I do. What I did. You're just another plus one,' says Vince. 'Pop, pop.'

Vince slowly saunters towards Harvey without any hint of fear. The Guinness has settled and looks like the perfect pint with the black stuff glistening underneath a creamy inch-thick head. Harvey is holding his own beer. In his giant hands, the pint pot looks like a chaser glass. Is he about to smash the glass into Vince's face? Does he know Vince might be armed?

Cain is waiting for the two giants to combust into an orgy of unrestrained violence. Vince picks up the Guinness and starts to neck it slowly and deliberately, giving Harvey every chance to throw the first punch.

Harvey watches him drink it, never moves an inch. The pint finished, Vince places it carefully on the wooden bar top and licks the cream from his top lip like he is Mel Sykes or Anna Chancellor in one of those famous ads on TV during Boddingtons *Cream of Manchester* heyday.

'You can go now ex-detective Leonard Harvey, you've got no reason to be on these premises and we're closed out of respect for Cain's fiancée. Say nighty night to Cain. And do the opposite of that Dylan Thomas poem, do go gentle into that good — and silent, very silent, say nothing silent — night.'

Any moment Cain expects a reaction — any reaction — from the former detective, his old friend and drinking buddy who has always managed to intimidate and amuse him in the same breath. Except Harvey looks old, like Ali and Liston and Tyson when they were spent punch-drunk boxers, shells of their awesome prime-time selves.

'Can I finish my pint?' asks Harvey.

'Sure. You're paying for it because I am buying this place when Cain flies off to America with April,' says Vince.

There is another short stand-off while Harvey downs his pint and exposes his neck for an attack. He places the pint gently on the bar and pulls ten quid from his pocket and puts it under the glass.

'I had two pints.'

'You need another two quid.'

Harvey delves into the pocket of his black trousers, produces a couple of coins and plops them on the bar and tips his hat to Vince and Cain before grabbing a bottle of Macallan Classic Cut 2017 whisky from the shelf behind the bar.

'A 'thank you' present from Cain for all I did for you. You

should be careful what you wish for and pick your friends very carefully. We'll toast the spirit of Jimmy Bone, knicker sniffer turned pedigree chum. Don't be a Jimmy, Vince.'

'I am a winner, not a loser, like Jimmy Bone,' says Vince.

'Sure, that's what Jimmy said to me once,' says Harvey, who walks slowly up to Cain and shakes his hand and whispers to him to leave ASAP and let Vince lock up the Manifesto. 'The cops are coming.'

Once Harvey exits, Vince walks towards Cain, the gun tucked into the front of his trousers, the plastic black grips clearly visible.

'I am sorry about Lucy Button,' says Cain.

'Don't be. She is a heroin addict and knew she risked death every time she tried to find a corner to inject Billy's poison into her arms. He is the biggest supplier of heroin in the city.'

'I thought he was against Class A?'

'PR bullshit. Forget Lucy. I am telling you straight, no bullshit attached, Billy McGinty is behind the attack on April and you by the canal. He is also responsible for Lucy's rape and murder. He wanted dirt on April to blackmail her so she would gift him the Red Manifesto, but Lucy stayed true to her friend.'

'Killing someone for a bloody restaurant? For bloody bricks and mortar and a bit of brand building? Risk life imprisonment?'

'Billy encouraged Lucas Bone and Ryan McGinty to sexually assault her, then they gave her a fatal overdose of pure heroin before burning any evidence,' said Vince.

'What dirt?'

'About Billy driving the car. April knew because Violet is her best friend, and she was sat next to Billy when they killed Hannah.'

'Why did Lucy and April slap each other?'

'Lucy was scared April would tell you about Billy killing your daughter. Billy would blame her and punish her, try and punish me too, but that's a fight he would not win.'

'How do I know you're telling me the truth?'

'The black Golf is buried in his farm in Simister. Dug a big hole with an excavator and hid his and Violet's secret. That big pond. The landscaped golf hole. It's somewhere there.'

'Still?'

'As far as I know, yes. Billy paid Ted Blake to take the blame for him. Knew Ted was dying. Promised to take care of his family in return. Dot gets weekly wages as a bookkeeper looking after Violet's brothels. A good gig for her.'

'That's a lot to take in Vince,' said Cain, unsure what he could believe from Vince's monologue.

'It's very simple Cain. For years Billy's ruled the roost. Everyone is too scared to say dick to him. And they have every reason to be. He's a psychopath. You don't question Billy or negotiate with him. There's only one language he understands. Violence. In his world, it's the only thing that makes any sense. You can only answer his violence with more terrifying violence. You must be nastier. More ruthless, let your dogs rip a man to pieces in front of his friends in a squash court. Your dogs do it quicker and nastier.'

'Did that really happen?'

'Jimmy Bone. I saw it with my own eyes. Harvey was there too. He was the bloody referee.'

Vince pulls out the gun and holds it momentarily to Cain's head and pulls it away again just as quickly and laughs out loud.

'Bloody hell Vince.'

'Only messing with you, the safety is on. It is me who fired the air rifle at you just now. That was a laugh, you shouting, 'come on'. Billy McGinty killed your daughter. The proof is at his farm, bring a bucket and a spade. You can have instant revenge for a price.'

'Price?'

'The Red Manifesto, lock, stock and barrel. Shake on it.'

'I'll need April's daughter's signature too, most of it belongs to her as she is the next of kin,' says Cain, unsure if he should spell out his ninety/ten split means he has very little say in anything apart from designing a logo and posting online content. That makes him a lot less interesting to the Irishman.

'Your word is fine. April's already agreed to my offer to takeover the ownership.'

'When?'

'Sunday.'

'What time?'

'Sunday bloody Sunday is all you need to know.'

Yet another secret April has kept from him, unless...

'Before or after?'

'No hard feelings, just business.'

Vince offers Cain his hand, but the Irishman looks past him. Cain follows his eyes and sees the front door open, and Nick Forti walks in.

'We're closed, no barnstorming tonight, no free food either so take a hike, pal,' says Vince. 'Illegal immigrants or asylum seekers aren't welcome here.'

'Nick's a friend,' says Cain.

'Can we chat, Cain, privately,' says Nick.

'Nick 'Thor' Forti,' says Cain.

'You've not aged well Nick,' says Vince. 'Missing them pegs.'

'Can still throw a punch to knock you out cold,' says Nick. 'One arrow with your glass chin.'

'Sure, you can, wee fella,' says Vince, exposing the pistol in his belt as he zips up his leather jacket. 'Yours fists versus my bullets. Not a real contest. What are you doing here?'

'Said I'd walk Cain home in case three big boys attack him again.'

'That's good of you, Nick. Your reward is more salacious threesomes with Summer replacing her mum? Sexy or. Nancy Hood pays top dollar for juicy tit bits.'

'Whatever, Vincent,' says Nick.

Cain asks Vince to lock up the Manifesto, check all the doors and windows, ensure everything is secured.

'Be your place soon Vince, if your plans work out,' says Cain, seeing the real Vince grin back at him for the first time. Nick said there were three attackers on the towpath that night. Cain thought Nick was asking April to count his fingers, but he was talking mugger numbers. Three attackers and threesomes in the bed, Nancy's source cannot help bragging and revealing himself, needs to prove how clever and tough he is. Was Vince blackmailing April? Was that why she had to tell him about Blake not being the driver? Finally facing up to the truth?

Twenty-two

Outside the Manifesto, Nick excitedly tells Cain he's been visiting his old haunts, gyms and boxing clubs he frequented when he was an active pugilist, telling anyone who cares to listen that he is desperate to reunite with his ex-wife Kylie by going down on one knee with a knock out engagement ring like the one that celebrity chef was given by her lanky boyfriend. He has cash and needs it ASAP, to prove to her Nick 'Thor' Forti is back in business.

Cain thanks him for his efforts as they stroll along the towpath, says it is a long shot, but it was worth a punt to see if his ring turned up. Made sense that genuine muggers would off-load it as soon as possible with fellow thieves and vagabonds.

Nick shakes his head and grins a toothless grin and hands Cain an engagement ring.

'I found it. Dead chuffed with myself.

Cain glances at it and knows it isn't the ring, except he is too shattered to disappoint Nick, who is really pleased with his good detective work and negotiating skills.

Nick says his mate Diamond Dave has agreed four grand cash. He needs two more tomorrow, but DD trusts him enough to give him the ring in advance.

Nick thanks him and says Kylie will love the story when he tells her about reuniting Cain with his engagement ring, says it will give him an excuse to call her and start rebuilding his life.

Cain nods and knows telling Nick he's been conned will damage his fragile confidence and make him feel a fool.

They walk a bit further down the towpath to the staircase accessed via Castle Street, the exact spot where April and Cain were attacked on Sunday night. Cain stops and glances around.

'The two of them were waiting for us, a planned not random attack.'

'Three. There were three attackers, not two. I told you at the time.'

'You saw them clearly?'

'No really. Two of them went towards Deansgate Locks, the third back up to Castle Street.'

'Did the third look like Vince Crane?'

'Don't know. I wasn't wearing my distance glasses.'

'Have you got any?'

'No. You have nothing when you're homeless. Not vision or self-respect. You've given me that back by trusting me,' says Nick.

They walk some more and stop again under the bridge that leads up to Deansgate. Cain is going to have a smoke before heading to the flat. He offers Nick a tab, but he refuses, says he is going to go back into training, get himself fighting fit and mentor young kids to box smart, not throw wild west haymakers and hope for the best. Once he tells Kylie, she will be back onside.

'Have you got kids?'

'Two. Girl and a boy. Molly and Noel.'

'If somebody hurt them, what would you do?'

'Hurt them back twice as hard.'

'Kill them?'

Nick cracks his knuckles one by one instead of replying spontaneously. Cain blows a smoke ring over the canal and watches it expand and disappear.

'You think Billy is the third man who attacked April?' asks Nick.

'Yes. And Vince says Billy drove the car that killed my daughter two decades ago.'

'Shit.'

'Would you?'

'Do you believe in the death penalty?' asks Nick.

'No.'

'Why.'

'If one murder is wrong, all murders are wrong.'

'There's your answer,' says Nick.

'If you were wearing my shoes, would you go to America with April or stay here and seek justice?'

'You'll be giving me a migraine with all these questions,' replies Nick. 'Should you go after Billy McGinty for what he did to you? Only if you've got a death wish. I refused to take a dive for him, and he busted my marriage with an elongated honey-trapping scam that included hooking me on junk. I'd walk away from him. He's toxic. Nasty. Saw him slash somebody's face open with a bottle because he bumped into him at a bar in Salford. You don't want to get in the ring with him. He'll infect you with his hatred and his violence.'

'Walk away?'

'Too right. Forgive him. You're a better man than him

festering away in a prison of his own making. Spends his whole life looking over his shoulder, waiting for a man like Vince to try and kill him. You want to be him?'

They walk under the bridge with graffiti covering the walls and dim LED lights give the corridor a ghostly glow. As they near the end, a huge figure steps out and blocks their path.

'OK, Cain. A private word, can you give us ten minutes, my friend.'

Cain nods and says to Nick he'll see him back at the apartment. He and Len are old friends and have some catching up to do. Nick asks several times if Cain is sure, and each time he says yes. Finally convinced, Nick leaves and walks towards Deansgate, without looking back.

Cain and Harvey wait for Nick to step out of earshot.

'Nick 'Thor' Forti?'

'Yes.'

'Spirited fighter. Too brave for his own good.'

'A good egg. Saved mine and April's bacon on Sunday.'

Harvey delves into an inside pocket of his large overcoat and brings out the Macallan Classic Cut 2017 whisky. Unscrews the top from the bottle and takes a deep swig and hands it to Cain.

'That's an eight hundred quid bottle,' says Cain, letting the warm single malt swill around his mouth before swallowing. 'Have you called the cops?'

'Any officer, current or former, would be worried about sloppy Vince strutting around a restaurant with his gun down his trousers. He's got about ten minutes of freedom left. At least he'll live to collect his IRA pension, unless he starts blabbing about his old friends too. By the way it wasn't Billy. Vince is lying to you about Billy killing Hannah.'

'How do you know?'

'Because Billy was still in France when Hannah was

killed. I was becoming his friend if you know what I mean, 'fundraising' to finish their film and be forever in my debt. Best bit of fishing I ever did. I'll deny it and if you gossip about Billy, he will kill you like Jimmy Bone. I won't be able to protect you.'

'I've seen the DVD extras on *All Down the Line*. The black Golf is there with the girls and Ted climbing out of it. That's the car you could not find. April is getting out of the...driver's side of a European left-hand drive.'

'Destroyed or burned out. We'll never know.'

'Vince says it is buried at Billy's farm.'

'Vince talks shit.'

'April doesn't drive because of her eyesight,' says Cain, and the final lie slots into place but he cannot say the words.

Cain's legs go from underneath and Harvey bear hugs him to stop him collapsing into a heap on the concrete.

'Put it in a box and slam the lid shut and never open it again. Remember that movie with Jack Nicholson. The famous ending: Forget it, Jake. It's Chinatown! You can't change anything. Swap Chinatown for Manchester.'

'What are you trying to say?'

'Leave it all alone. Don't cross that line.'

'Why?'

'Because you'll end up as dog meat, like Jimmy Bone,' says Harvey.

'That's anecdotal, surely.'

'Jimmy broke Billy's code of conduct and paid for it big time. I was there to oversee a fist fight except Billy brought his dogs. Vince was there too, in Jimmy's corner. Half a dozen other shadowland faces.'

'And you let Billy get away with murder as a police officer?' asks Cain.

'If they killed each other fighting, I am fine with that. As long as no civilians are hurt. We police by consensus in

Manchester and if it isn't them, it would be somebody else who is king of the underworld. At least Billy is uncomplicated.'

'And Hannah? Is she 'one of them'?'

'Of course not,' says Harvey.

'What about me? I am a civilian too?' And April? Is she a civilian?'

'You need to discuss it with her, not me.'

'That's difficult at the moment.'

'This conversation is over Cain. Vince Crane's off your back. Don't destroy yourself out of false pride and anger.'

'Did Vince attack us on Sunday?'

'Wasn't Billy,' said Harvey.

'His son was involved.'

'You know what families are like.'

Cain was stumped, Harvey is right. This is Castlefield, Manchester, the shadowlands, they do things differently here. They ruin lives and cover up bad deeds.

'What was in it for you, Len? Why did you cross the line and get dirty?'

'I believe in poetic justice. You should too. Truth is overrated. Believe me, son,' says Harvey. 'All violence ends with a truce.'

They shake hands and go their separate ways, Cain up onto Deansgate and Harvey back down towards the Basin where he has presumably parked his car.

Cain has already decided he is going by himself tomorrow under his own steam, nobody buys him off or owns him. At the top, he waits on the bridge and looks down the Rochdale Canal tow path towards the basin and the Red Manifesto.

Harvey is making his way there slowly without a care in the world.

Suddenly dozens of blue lights are flashing outside the restaurant April has built and destroyed.

Harvey is right, the cops are coming. How will Vince

react? Cain hopes the armed response shoot him dead like the vermin he is but the prick is more than likely going to surrender and cut a deal.

Twenty-three

When Cain arrives back in his apartment, Nick, Bob and
Summer are in the sitting room watching Bob Mitchum in
The Friends of Eddie Coyle about a low-level grass about to
be wiped out by a mate for snitching to the cops about gun
running. Cain loves the slow-burn film and has watched it at
least half dozen times over the decades, the sadness of the
inevitably of the assassination obvious to everyone except
Eddie. Cain has an online library of over a thousand digital
films that encapsulates who he is and how he feels about
life. Same with his online digital music collection. His life
stored in a cloud and accessed anywhere in the world on a
device the same size as a bar of soap. Nick asks if he is OK
and Cain says everything is fine, although he is shattered. He
thanks him for the ring and coming out to meet him but is
distracted mid-sentence when he glances out of the window

to see the Castlefield Basin awash with blue flashing lights forming a semi-circle outside the Manifesto.

'What's going on?' asks Bob.

'Haven't a clue,' lies Cain. 'If it is anything to do with us the police will get in touch soon enough.'

'Maybe some goons are trying to rob the place,' says Nick.

'Have you eaten?' asks Summer.

She sounds just like her mum, April, always checking Cain is well fed, realising that food is an equally accessible route to a man's heart as a bed, or a sofa or standing up in the hall, like they do in the movies whenever the script is running out of steam and the story needs a salacious lift.

'Not hungry. Any news on your mum?'

'They've stopped giving her sedation drugs. She could come out of her coma anytime tomorrow,' says Summer.

'Or not,' says Cain.

'Any movement, the slightest flicker or flinch, shows she's alive.'

'So they say,' says Cain.

'It will be a tiny miracle when she comes out of her coma,' says Summer.

Does he tell Summer the truth or kick the can down the road and let someone else do the dirty deed? Is that his responsibility as an adult to add to her heartache? Or does he just take off and disappear without an explanation, vanish into the wind like a smoke ring blown out over a canal?

Although he owes Nick, there is no obligation to placate Summer and Bob beyond disentangling himself from the Red Manifesto. To do that he has to unlock April safe in his bedroom and intrude into his former fiancée's documented world. He doesn't know what he will find, but he can take what he needs, and hand over the combination and contents to Summer and Bob. April's worldly goods belong to them, not to him. Like a forgotten overdue library book, his love expired without him knowing and needed to be returned before the fine spirals out of control.

That's all bollocks.

Bottom line: he no longer wants to be complicit in April's lies?

Big question: does he need a witness when he opens April's safe to ensure he behaves and isn't tempted to take what isn't his?

'Come with me for five minutes,' says Cain to Summer.

Inside the bedroom, Cain goes to far left-hand corner of the wall-to-wall, floor-to-ceiling mirrored fitted wardrobe. Like the split in the ownership of the Red Manifesto, ninety per cent is for April's clothes, ten for his.

He opens the mirrored doors and takes down his ten-year old sandy yellow ruck sack and throws it on the bed.

'What are you doing?' asks Summer.

'Packing,' says Cain, chucking assorted jumpers and jackets, tee shirts and jeans and socks and underwear onto the bed.

'Why?'

'This isn't my home, it's yours.'

'You're engaged to my mum.'

'Was.'

'What's changed?'

'Everything,' says Cain.

He goes to the other end of the wardrobe and opens the door and the pretend shoe cupboard with a safe behind it.

'I don't understand.'

'While April's incapacitated, you're responsible for her legal and financial affairs. If she dies, you'll be responsible for managing her estate or at least overseeing it. Professionals can help you with probate. I looked after my parents' affairs when they died. They didn't have enough to employ lawyers and accountants.'

Cain empties the safe, leaving the cash and jewellery boxes. He places the contents on a writing table that overlooks Deansgate.

'I don't want you go,' cries Summer. 'What have I done wrong? Is it the praying? I'll stop. Is the International Redemption Agency? I can leave.'

'No. It's me,' says Cain, rifling through the documents, deciding if he has a right to read April's private correspondence. 'I need to move on or I'll fall into a void.'

There is a large A4 enveloped addressed to April from California dated early Spring the previous year. Inside is a very short letter from Bob to April refusing to sign the divorce papers. He does not give a reason. Cain looks through the paperwork. April has signed both but needs Bob's and two witnesses to sign and date the documents.

'Can I see?'

Cain hands her the divorce papers.

Another envelope is addressed to Bob and contains the deeds to the apartment. He owns it all, registered only in his name, complete financial control over his estranged wife who cannot blink without his permission.

A third envelope has the share certificates for the Red Manifesto, forty per cent Bob, thirty per cent April, thirty per cent...Billy McGinty. Cain owns ten percent of April's thirty and has paid her a hundred and forty grand for the privilege, way over the odds. She has stitched him good and proper, ripped him off like a professional grifter. The ownership makes a mockery of Vince's suggestion that Billy McGinty wants to buy into the Red Manifesto. McGinty already has a large chunk, a majority share for him and Bob if they are in already cahoots and ripping off him and the taxpayers with dodgy deals.

Another envelope contains contracts for her publishing deals and agents, forty or so individual deals he doesn't have time to skim let alone read, share certificates for others Manchester businesses co-owned with her husband and Billy McGinty.

There are four more envelopes. One addressed to Cain, 'to be opened upon my death', a similar letter with the same message addressed to Summer and two large brown cardboard-backed envelope, one marked 'happy', the other 'sad & bad'. The latter has ten photographs of the top halves of April and Violet in bras, beaten and bruised. On the back of each picture, a handwritten note of the date and the perpetrators, sometimes Bob, sometimes Billy, sometimes both. The abuse dates start in 2001 and stop in 2014, a year before she hooked up with Cain

'Jesus.'

'Jesus.'

'We should open the letters addressed to us.'

'She's not dead yet,' says Cain.

'You're right,' replies Summer.

Cain opens the 'happy' envelope and pull out three photographs of April, Summer and Ryan smiling and hugging each other. On the back are the locations and dates of their gatherings: Heaton Park (2013), Prestwich Clough (2014) and Blackpool (2015).

'What's going on?' asks Cain, knowing exactly what is going down but playing dumb for appearances. 'This is the youth who attacked me and April? Left her for dead. You know him?'

'Is that the first of your six questions? You might need more.'

'Stop messing with my head.'

'We look a lot like twins who take after our birth mother. Ryan's my brother and my protector. My mum told me about him when I stabbed my dad in the neck with the cross around my neck. That scar on his neck, that's me. You think the cross is burnished with red paint as a symbolic decoration. It's the bastard's blood. I saw him hit my mother two or three times and I defended her. Stopped her the only way I knew how. Stopped him beating on her by cutting his flesh. Reminded him to behave. My involvement with the International Redemption Agency reminds him to behave because he believes in the power of prayer to ruin him. You cannot beat a cult.'

'When?'

'We were in Manchester on a holiday. We took the old man to hospital to get stitched up and she told me about France and Ryan. I could meet him, but it would have to stay a secret otherwise Billy... I swore on our lives.'

'Ryan knows too?'

'Last time Billy and Bob beat her and Violet, my mum decided to play ball and pretended she was an obedient little woman. Billy told her Ryan and Summer could never meet otherwise he'd Jimmy Bone her. She swore blind that would never happen and then walked up to Ryan in the street on the way back from school and introduced herself as his birth mother and told him about me.'

'Just like that?'

'She'd rather die than deny him or me. He believed her when she showed him my picture,' says Summer.

'Does she explain why?'

'Mum felt sorry for Violet when her baby was stillborn in France and she was told she couldn't have any more children.'

'So just the three of you?'

'No.'

'Violet?' asks Cain.

'First time I met her is outside the hospital the other day but I can tell by her face she knows. How, you'd have to ask her or mum.'

'Our attack.'

'Ask Ryan, he says they are playing the long game.'

'What does that mean?'

'Karma takes care of bad people. Billy has leukaemia and needs a bone marrow transplant. Ryan's the obvious choice except...'

'Hung by his own petard? What do we do now?'

'Carry on looking after each other?'

'You don't need me,' says Cain.

'My mum does and so I.'

Cain wants to ask her about her mother killing Hannah, except he knows truth hurts and she does not need the pain. Harvey was right. People are always disingenuous, it's human instinct to portray yourself in the best possible light. Like he's never told anyone he should have been looking after Hannah better, not pissing about on his mobile arranging a rendezvous with a woman he met in a club a couple of nights before. He doesn't even remember her name or what she looks like. It's his big secret that constantly follows him and never leaves his mad shadows.

Twenty-four

Cain approaches the intensive care unit aware he doesn't have to do this. His backpack is packed, and he has a single ticket to Berlin to start a new life. He'll take a few days to acclimatise to a new city before he looks for work to occupy his mind.

He presses the buzzer to the secure unit, enters and swings the heavy backpack off his shoulders and sits down beside April, takes hold of her hand and flinches. This is going to be an awkward one-way conversation.

Staff nurse Cathy Moore, who is looking after April one-on-one, comes across and checks he is OK. He says yes and asks if April is off her medication. Cathy confirms they have stopped her sedation drugs.

'She's been to hell and back even before the brain bleed.

Blind in one eye. A still born baby cut out from her stomach at the same time as her womb is whipped out stopping her having any more children,' says Cain, spinning her narrative more to himself than Cathy stood beside him.

'That's odd. There's nothing on her records about blindness, caesareans or hysterectomies,' replies Cathy.

'Maybe I got it a little bit wrong,' says Cain, knowing one lie attracted more lies until they are all drowned in a tsunami of lies. 'I don't know her as well as I thought I did. We were only together for a short while. Any news about the family's cryonics wishes?'

'Freezing brain dead people isn't on our curriculum,' says Cathy.

'Thank God for common sense,' says Cain. 'Once the power is cut, it's over.'

Alone again, Cain strokes April's hand, still ice cold to the touch. They are still keeping the temperature in the room low.

'Why, April? Bob's signed the papers so you'll be divorced soon. The American dream and the Californian deep freeze are over, so you need to wake up one day. We both saw the photographs, good and bad. You and Violet suffering at the hands and fists of your husbands. Why couldn't you share your suffering? There is no embarrassment or humiliation involved. Why did you hide Summer and Ryan from me? Don't you trust me? Thought I was no different to the other men who hurt you? That hurts me so much.'

How dumb does that sound? Women don't voluntary surrender to men who are terrorising them. They — she — have no choice. Boxing pundits say big beats small, same as a heavier man always trumps a weaker woman. Their only safe defence is to run away, not so easy if you're skint and have children to look after.

Cain reaches into the pocket of his jeans and brings out

the wrong ring and toys with it before putting it back in his pocket. He still hasn't plucked up the courage to tell Nick about his error. His new mate is in reconciliation mode and doesn't need to be made to look foolish.

Cain places three fingers in April's palm, while his other hand strokes the back of her hand. She squeezes his three fingers. Very gently, barely noticeable, just the once. A tiny squeeze for him with life-affirming implications for April.

She is alive. Unlike their relationship. That is dead. Means he has the moral right to read the letter.

Cain opens the envelope, takes out an A4 sheet of paper folded into a third A4. She'd handwritten it a couple of months ago.

July 2017

Dear Cain

If you're reading this, I am dead and I still haven't had the courage in life to confess my sins to you. I've run away from a cruel world that's tortured me for the huge mistakes I've made, the lies I've told and the truth that I've deliberately hidden from you for nearly twenty years and continued to hide from you when we were one.

Now I am gone, I can share the worst of me with you. I was the driver who killed your daughter. For years you were told it was Ted Blake behind the wheel. But that was a lie, partly down to me wanting to save my own skin and ease my conscience.

I am sorry, so sorry, for ruining your life and killing your little girl. If I could swap places with her, you know I would.

I relive her death every day, never goes away. I was exhausted, driving up from Dover to Manchester but that was no consolation to you. I didn't see the lights on red at the pelican crossing next to the Forresters pub. I didn't see her walking out into the road in her little red dress carrying a pizza box and I didn't react to Violet's scream from the back seat where she was looking after MY babies.

A second's loss of concentration was all it took. Violet said we had to carry on until we reached the safety of her farm in Simister where Jimmy Bone was waiting for us in the half-light to unload the drugs we were smuggling, and we could look after our — MY — two kids. I was to shocked to think and did as I was told.

Why didn't I stop? I asked myself that question every single day when I replayed the crash. If I'd stopped, you'd have known who did it and I'd have gone to prison for manslaughter and not stopping at the scene of a fatal accident and Billy and Violet could have had both my kids rather than just one of them. Your life would have been completely different if I'd had the courage to face up to my crimes. I wanted to confess the day after the accident, but didn't, couldn't, wouldn't.

You know I gave my son away on the spur of the moment act of kindness because I felt so sorry for Violet who was told she'd never have kids again. A spontaneous gesture for all the right reasons, but totally stupid. And when I changed my mind, Bob and Billy said it was too late to alter the records they'd falsified, and money had changed hands to ensure All Down the Line was finished ready for release. I had no longer had rights over my child. What had started out as a good deed from me to my friend had become sinister and evil and unforgiveable. Bob said we had sold our baby to Billy and Violet to fund our film. The two of them swore me, Violet and Jimmy Bone to absolute secrecy on pain of death. That was meant to be a joke, but Billy was deadly serious, as Jimmy Bone found out. Whenever I spoke to Bob about Ryan, he would shush me up, sometimes he'd hit me and demand my absolute silence, said Billy would hurt him too if it got out. I asked Billy more than once to give me my son back and each time he hurt me bad until I promised never to mention my Ryan again. But I broke that promise and I found a way for them — Summer and him — to know each other.

I talked about you all the time with the psychiatrist Lucy Button. Lucy said you couldn't even start grieving when you were so fixated on finding the driver at the expense of everything and everybody else. Lucy, despite her drug problems, was a good friend to me and said when she'd comforted you in bed you'd cried and cried. I always wanted to tell you, but she always stopped me, said it would not do anybody any good. Foolishly I believed her, but that's no excuse for my callous behaviour.

A few months after the hit and run, I finally came up with a great idea. We could pay Ted Blake to confess because he was going to die anyway from cancer, and he could carry the can for me and his widow would get money every month for the rest of her life. Billy and Bob said they had a police mate who could make it real. They said the security man on All Down the Line was a detective during the day. I thought it would work out best for all of us and I suppose it did until you suddenly left Manchester, still unable to cope with your loss. I followed you from a distance online and via social media for years and years while you roamed like a hapless stray dog looking for a home. I contrived to meet you in Farsund, Norway, but that's a different happier story that I hope you can cherish if you can forgive me for my crimes against you and Hannah.

Not that it matters. I am dead. You know the truth. And I am truly, truly sorry, from the bottom of my broken heart. Nothing I can do can change what I have done, but I hope this letter makes life easier for you.

Love you forever & ever

April xxxx

PS: look after Summer for me — guide her, like you guided me.

What does he do with the letter? Does he feel clean, rinsed of all his worries?

'Everything OK?' asks Cathy Moore.

'Sure,' says Cain, 'I think she squeezed my hand. Just the once. She's coming out of her coma.'

'Show me what you did,' says Cathy with a huge cheesecake grin.

Cain goes through the motions for Cathy's sake but feels numb and detached from the skin-on-skin contact. He feels like saying April has responded to her confession and not his touch. Poor unknowing Cathy with her bright red hair and engaging reassuring smiles doesn't realise April is a killer and no longer Cain's best friend. A couple who lost and loved and lost again have discarded their future together. Wedding plans won't take place in Los Angeles, California, Manchester, or anywhere on this ridiculous spinning rock. There will be no honeymoon videos of a romantic road trip from Ventura Boulevard to Baja in Mexico, soundtracked by Lynyrd Skynyrd's *Tuesday's Gone*, Tom Petty's *Free Falling* and Creedence Clearwater Revival's *Have You Ever Seen the Rain*. Optimistic uplifting sad songs, if there was such a genre. There probably is. Cain won't call Shelley North and make plans for an exotic themed cookbook featuring indigenous and Tex Mex cuisine cooked in deserts under blood red skies. Summer wouldn't be the maid of honour giving her mother away, nor would she meet up with them in

Baja at the end of their epic west coast topless car journey. There is nothing left. Love is unconditional, until it isn't.

'Cain, I felt it too. That's brilliant news. Shall I go and call Summer or do you want to call her? Better coming from family.'

'You do it. I need some fresh air,' says Cain. 'Might grab a coffee, it's all too emotional.'

He leaves the ICU unit and sits on the bench underneath all the marketing posters boasting about the brilliance of the hospital and how prevention is better than cure. Out of nowhere a thirty-year-old pregnant woman comes and sits down next to him. She is wearing a little red dress, black tights and, like Helen of Troy, a gentle smile to launch a thousand ships.

'Hi. Don't move or speak. I am OK where I am. I am happy. You're not going to leave Summer by herself. She's just a kid, like I was once. You must take responsibility too, you know. If she was me, what would you do for her?'

Before Cain can reply, his dead daughter is gone. Just his imagination running away with him, again. All this pressure on him in life and from beyond the grave demanding he stands tall and refuses to run away.

He takes the phone from his pocket and rings Summer and leaves a message.

'Your mother's alive. She squeezed my hand. Are you coming down?'

As Cain finishes his call a lanky youth sits down beside him, looks a lot like Summer and April.

'Hello Ryan.'

'Cain.'

'How was Berwick?

'A red herring. We never went. I saw you in Lucy's bedroom. Glad you got out OK. Summer likes you. They both need you,' said Ryan.

'Your old man's the elephant in the room, dictates what happens next.'

'Does he?' asks Ryan. 'Billy's a nostalgia act who got lucky with my non-birth mum understanding how money works. She's the brains in the family.'

'Meaning?'

'The King is dead, long live Queen Violet and her black Prince, me' said Ryan.

'Sounds logical, not,' said Cain.

'Billy will be splashed all over news today for all the right and wrong reasons. Enough of him, Summer told me about your daughter. Sorry to hear about Hannah.'

'A long time ago.'

'Hit and run?'

'Yes.'

'Did they catch the driver?'

'No, Ted Blake died before the police could arrest him.'

'A shame, but as dead Mr Manchester Tony Wilson famously once said, *when forced to pick between the truth and the legend, print the legend.*'

'He's a wise man, knew how to sell a story and big himself up.'

'You know the real truth, Cain, forget the legend. My mum told Lucy Button she was going to confess everything to you, about giving me away for both altruistic and financial reasons and about her driving the car on that awful night, her words, not mine. Vince intercepted her on the towpath last Sunday to stop her blabbing after his blackmail attempt to steal your restaurant backfired big time.'

'Who hit her? You or Vince?'

'She fell when Vince pushed her and she hit her head on the ground. I was meant to be protecting her and failed.'

'Why didn't tell you the police?'

'You're a funny man for an old git. This belongs to you

and my birth mum. Vince stole it. I stole it back for you when she gets better,' said Ryan and he hands Cain his engagement ring. Cain looks at the princess cut diamond solitaire ring set in 18 carat yellow gold.

It is the real deal, some karma talking, warm and sweet.

Death is not the End

Silence. Absolute silence. The dogs aren't barking. Have they gone on hunger strike? There's another ditty about death, where Dylan sings death is not the end, even if you're sad, lonely, and without a friend. Fantasy bollocks, isn't it? The farmhouse should be empty apart from me, but I can hear movement. I should react, but I am tired of looking over my shoulder all my life. Being top dawg is an isolating experience. They may hate you, they may fear you, they may even respect you, but they'll never like and love you. Out over the balcony, blue lights are flashing towards the farm. Is Vince spilling the beans about Jimmy Bones and all the others? Is he going to be a grass like me? Len says they nicked him with a pistol down his pants like *Johnny Too Bad*. Will he cut a deal with Dibble, like I did with Harvey in 1997? I can hear the slight creaking of soft shoes on a badly installed staircase. Bloody Jimmy

Bone is a carpenter by trade, like Jesus, except he was always cutting corners. The door opens and I can see his son, Lucas, with a gun in his hand and suicide on his mind. He asks if I want to write a goodbye note. I tell him, like Sonny Liston, I cannot read or write, why else did I become a gangster? It was never a lifestyle choice, more a necessity. Who the fuck is Sonny Liston, asks Lucas, he'll have him any day. He tells me it's nothing personal, like they all do, copying the movies. He's crying and says bloody Ryan stitched him up. There are videos of him masturbating over a stiff on the internet and the whole wide world can see his face. I almost laugh, but stop, brace myself for the void. *Sing Me Back Home*, as Merle would croon...death IS the end, no questions asked.

Author's Note

All Down the Line was first published in December 2020. Earlier that year the Covid pandemic broke out in the UK and our lives would never be the same again. A year earlier I left Manchester to live by the sea in Northumberland and *Line* was my farewell to the brilliant city where I'd spent most of my adult life. When I revisited the book to publish a hardcover version last year, minor revisions evolved into a more extensive rewrite. Although I loved the original narrative arc and all the characters, the world has changed so much in five years and our heroes no longer automatically win, nor does justice prevail, although 'karma' always has its way. Truth and facts no longer matter in a polarised world where disingenuous billionaire big mouths rule the waves. Sooner or later, democracy will have its day in the sun again – but only if we make sure we never give the belligerent buggers an easy ride and call them out whenever they lie, steal and cheat.

Andrew J Field, 2025

Always Adam by Mark Brumby

London-based financial journalist Spencer Beck is obsessed with billionaire biotech prodigy, Adam Reid, orphaned in his mid-teens when his parents died in a tragic murder-suicide in New York City. A shadowy informant with MI5 connections promises Beck unfettered access to the mysterious Reid and introduces him to Daniel Flanagan, a retired Big Apple detective who investigated the deaths of Adam's mother and father. Spencer's initial scepticism, fed by the suspicions of the former police officer, turns to excitement when Reid reveals the truth about himself and his altruistic ambitions to protect society from a deadly virus with a powerful vaccine he's developed. But when Beck's entire world starts to implode, he discovers Reid harbours a vendetta that, left unchecked, threatens not only his survival but that of an entire species.

Big Daddy by Mark Brumby

Vikings wake in the tenth century and die in the twentieth. A Nazi platoon massacres civilians in Poland fifty years after Adolf Hitler's death. A B-29 bomber, lost in 1945, resumes a mission in 1999 to drop an atomic bomb on Tokyo. Big Daddy is larger than the Little Boy and Fat Man bombs that devastated Hiroshima and Nagasaki respectively. Now, at the turn of the 21st century, world leaders and scientists race against time to locate and neutralise the scientist behind a timeless flight where the future of humanity is hanging in the balance. Mark Brumby's Big Daddy is a masterful story packed full of suspense, science fiction ingenuity and historical intrigue.